The sun was an orange-red ball in a crimson sky that was deepening to purple. *Excessive.*

Jason veered toward his beach towel as a cool wind suddenly blew across the beach, making the hairs on his arms stand up. He shivered, feeling cold in the evening air. *Bevare the cold,* a little voice whispered in his head.

Jason ignored it. A cold wind in December was hardly something to worry about. He reached his beach towel and noted that his wetsuit was completely dry. He could just stuff it in his backpack. He leaned forward, bending his knees a little, to grab the pack—

Thunk! Jason felt something cold and hard slam into his body.

The impact forced him to stagger backwards. Red dots – like a dozen tiny setting suns – filled his vision for a moment. He blinked and looked down to see a thin metal bar sticking out of his chest . . .

www.kidsatrandomhouse.co.uk

VAMPIRE
BEACH

VAMPIRE BEACH
Ritual

Alex Duval

RED FOX BOOKS

Copyright © Working Partners Limited, 2007

The right of Alex Duval to be identified as the author of this work has been
asserted in accordance with the Copyright, Designs and Patents Act 1988.

Papers used by Random House Children's Books are natural, recyclable products
made from wood grown in sustainable forests. The manufacturing processes
conform to the environmental regulations of the country of origin.

Set in 12/16pt Minion by
FalconOast Graphic Art Ltd.

Red Fox Books are published by Random House Children's Books,
61–63 Uxbridge Road, London W5 5SA,
a division of The Random House Group Ltd,
in Australia by Random House Australia (Pty) Ltd,
20 Alfred Street, Milsons Point, Sydney, NSW 2061, Australia,
in New Zealand by Random House New Zealand Ltd,
18 Poland Road, Glenfield, Auckland 10, New Zealand,
in South Africa by Random House (Pty) Ltd,
Isle of Houghton, Corner Boundary Road & Carse O'Gowrie,
Houghton 2198, South Africa
and in India by Random House India Pvt Ltd, 301 World Trade Tower, Hotel
Intercontinental Grand Complex,
Barakhamba Lane, New Delhi 110001, India.

THE RANDOM HOUSE GROUP Limited Reg. No. 954009
www.kidsatrandomhouse.co.uk

A CIP catalogue record for this book is available from the British Library.

Printed and bound in Great Britain by
Bookmarque Ltd, Croydon, Surrey

For Deborah Rose Bramwell

Special thanks to Laura Burns & Melinda Metz

ONE

'Let's sign up for an angel reading!' Jason Freeman's little sister, Dani, exclaimed from the back seat of his 1975 Volkswagen Karmann Cabriolet. 'It says here that the psychic is in touch with the angels all around us and passes on information from them.'

Jason was chauffeuring Dani and her friend Kristy to the Arcana Psychic Fair, since neither of them was quite old enough to have a driver's license. He had agreed to do this only because Dani had promised to do his chores for three weeks in payment.

Their parents were in New York for some business thing of his dad's, so they couldn't take the girls to the fair. And Kristy's parents had given a big 'no way' when she had asked them to drive. Maria – Dani and Kristy's designated driver, who was a year older and had already taken driver's ed – was sick. That left Jason, who now had three sweet chore-free weeks to look forward to.

'The angel reading sounds good,' Kristy told Dani. 'But top of my list is one of those pictures where you can see your aura. You can tell which are your strong points – like creativity or a healing nature.'

'Yeah, and a picture would be a great souvenir too,' Dani agreed.

'I don't know if the aura picture is a good idea. Yours looks a little oily to me today,' Jason teased his sister. 'When's the last time you washed it?'

'You're being paid to drive, not talk,' Dani joked back, her chin-length auburn hair blowing round her face.

'I'm getting paid? All right. Because getting up at six on a Saturday morning is insane. Is there a reason this thing had to be out in the middle of the Mojave instead of right in our own Malibu?'

'The area near Joshua Tree has great spiritual vibrations,' Kristy explained.

Jason nodded. 'Well, I'm thinking that four weeks of chores isn't really enough to cover the early hour and the almost three-hour drive, so I'm glad you're throwing in some cash.' Not that driving down the highway through the desert was so bad. Jason loved driving the Bug, top down, on a nice, flat stretch of mostly empty road.

'*Three* weeks,' Dani protested, just the way Jason knew she would. 'Three weeks. Not four! That's your pay. That's what you agreed to and that is what you're getting. No money, no nothing else. And, actually, I think *two* weeks would be a lot more reasonable since you're getting to use Maria's ticket, which cost forty bucks.'

'Yeah. You're getting into the fair for free,' Kristy agreed. 'And the ticket includes one reading of your choice. You should knock off a week of chores for that.'

'That's OK,' Jason responded. 'I already know what the angels would say: *"Jason, you're so hot." "Jason, are we going to hook up at the next party?"* Stuff like that. I mean, that's what they say at school.'

'Cheeseball,' Dani muttered.

'You two can have the extra reading,' Jason said. 'I think I'll go get a coffee or something and pick you guys up later.'

'He thinks the whole psychic fair is silly,' Dani explained to her friend.

'Maria was in London over Thanksgiving and she said everyone there is really into the occult. Girls go get crystal therapy as often as manicures. Not that it's just a girl thing,' Kristy added quickly. 'We'll find you a good manly reading, Jason.'

He glanced in the rear-view mirror and saw Kristy and Dani leaning over the brochure for the fair – as if they didn't have it memorized by now.

'Tarot cards?' Dani murmured. 'Past-life regression? Channeling? Hmmm. Channeling. I want to try that. Maria said channelers can warn you about bad things that are going to happen to you, so that you can be prepared.'

Jason wasn't crazy about the sound of that. 'Guys, you know a fair like this is going to bring out a lot of people who are just after your money,' he said. 'I want you to have fun. But don't let anybody convince you to whip out your AmEx and pony up five hundred dollars for a charm of protection or love potion or something. Just think of the whole thing as entertainment, OK?'

'Don't you believe in *anything*, Jason?' Kristy asked.

'I believe in a lot of things,' Jason answered.

'Yeah,' Dani put in. 'You believe in surfing, and fish tacos at Eddie's, and your car, and—'

'Wait! Here's the perfect thing for your brother,' Kristy interrupted. 'It's a total guy thing. It's not a reading, but it says you can use a reading ticket.'

' "*A lecture that reveals the dark magic of vampires*",' Dani read over her friend's shoulder. She laughed.

'Kristy, we've got to start him out small. Maybe the lecture on herbal healing would be better. Jason's head will probably implode if he tries to accept that *vampires* exist.'

But the weird thing was that Jason did. He completely accepted it. Because, since moving from Michigan to DeVere Heights, Jason had found the body of a girl killed by a vampire, been attacked by a vampire, and made friends with a vampire. In fact, Jason had even fallen in love with a vampire, because the strange fact was that, here in DeVere Heights, all the coolest kids were vampires.

'There it is!' Kristy called out. 'The Joshua Tree Center for Mind, Body, and Spirit.'

There it is, and nothing else, Jason thought as he parked the Bug. He could forget about his plan of escaping for some coffee and down time. Unless he wanted to drive twenty miles back to that barely-a-town before the turn-off.

'You think they have coffee in there anyplace?' he asked the girls. 'Soda? A place where I can get caffeine injected directly into my heart?' Why had he agreed to do anything that involved getting up before noon on a Saturday?

'It says in the brochure that they have all kinds of food and stuff,' Kristy told him.

'Does that mean you're coming in?' Dani inquired.

'Lead the way,' Jason told her.

'I wonder if we'll see anyone from school here,' Dani said as they crossed the parking lot.

'Why would we? We're hours away from Malibu,' Jason pointed out. He definitely didn't want to be seen at the Arcana Psychic Fair. It's not that he didn't have an open mind. Or believe in *things*. But this was a completely woo-woo, touchy-feely kind of event at which no self-respecting guy should be seen.

'It's not like we're the only ones interested in this stuff,' Kristy said. 'And this is the biggest psychic fair in Southern California.'

'OK, let's get one thing straight. You see anyone from school, you give me a heads up, because I'll be struck with the sudden urge to use the bathroom. And no telling anyone I was here or I'll never drive either of you anywhere again. Got it?' Jason demanded.

Dani pulled the tickets out of her purse and thrust them at him. 'Fine,' she said. 'Like Kristy and I spend our time gossiping about *you* anyway.'

The two girls hurried into the big adobe building ahead of him. Jason handed the tickets to the guy at the door, shoved the stubs into his wallet and slowly followed the girls. The large cavern of a room was filled with row after row of booths, some selling stuff like herbs or books – one actually looked like it was selling *broomsticks* – some set up with people doing tarot readings or crystal gazing. Jason was surprised how normal many of the supposed psychics seemed. A lot of them were wearing jeans and shirts that could have come straight out of Gap.

And why shouldn't they? he asked himself. *Why should psychics wear headscarves and those long gauzy skirts?* After all, the vampires he knew looked like normal people. OK, incredibly popular, insanely good-looking normal people, but normal nonetheless. They didn't wear long black capes. They didn't have fangs unless they were drinking blood. And they didn't sleep in coffins or only come out at night. In fact, they didn't fall into any of the vampire clichés.

Jason headed after Dani and Kristy, not bothering to catch up to them. The air in the center seemed weighted down with the scent of candle wax, incense and old paper. But he could see equipment that looked ultra high-tech too, and massage tables that looked like they'd been pulled straight from a sports med clinic.

He paused at a booth that sold jewelry. There was

this one thing that grabbed him. A simple, perfectly round crystal, dark and iridescent, hanging from a slender silver chain. He could see Sienna wearing it – maybe even at the masked ball at Sandhurst Castle that was coming up, depending on her dress. But he knew it wasn't something he could buy her. He could maybe get away with giving her some goofy little thing, but that was it as long as she was with another guy. Which she was. Another guy, who also happened to be a friend of Jason's.

But that won't be forever, will it? Jason wondered. *They—*

'Jason, we thought you'd want to know,' Kristy said, appearing beside him and breaking into his thoughts. 'We just saw Belle Rémy heading over to talk to the guy who gives instruction on astral projection. That's just one row over.'

'And you know that where there's Belle Rémy, there's usually Sienna Devereux,' Dani added, her gray eyes sparkling. 'Now, are you still sure you don't want to see anyone from school? Because you usually like to see Sienna.'

'One row that way, or that way?' Jason asked, not sure if he wanted to know so that he could head toward or away from Sienna: a feeling he often had about her

– the girl he was in love with, even though he shouldn't be.

Dani and Kristy looked at each other and cracked up. And Jason realized he'd been had. By two little sophomores. He rolled his eyes. 'Very funny.'

'It was very funny,' Dani agreed. 'You should have seen your face.' She widened her eyes and let her mouth drop open, and she and Kristy cracked up again.

'Remember who drove you here,' Jason mock-threatened. 'Remember how far you'd have to walk to get home – through the desert, in your silly little shoes.'

They both ignored him. 'Oooh, I'm going to sign up for one of those massages,' Kristy said, looking over at a booth across the aisle. 'They don't even touch you. They just manipulate your energy field. It's supposed to make you feel amazing. You want me to put you down?' she asked Dani. 'Look how long the line is already.'

'I think I'd feel weird getting massaged in front of everybody like that,' Dani said. Jason nodded agreement, glancing at the masseur, who stood over a woman lying on the table in his small booth, plucking the air around her body as if he was playing the bass.

'That won't bother me,' Kristy answered. 'I'm going

to go and put my name down. Be right back.' She hurried over to the booth.

'So what is the deal with you and Sienna anyway?' Dani asked Jason. 'I've seen how you are together at parties, and sometimes even just in the hall at school. There's this vibe between you.'

'We're friends,' Jason told her. 'She was one of the first people I met when we moved here.'

Dani raised one eyebrow. 'And that's it? Friends?'

Jason shook his head. 'Dani, you know every detail about every person at DeVere High. That means you have to know that Sienna and Brad Moreau have been—'

'Together practically forever,' Dani finished for him. 'I know. But I also know what I see. And I see a vibe, and it's definitely not on the *friend* frequency.'

Jason knew where Dani was coming from. He did feel a more-than-friend vibe about Sienna, and he was pretty sure Sienna felt the same way about him, which is why they had ended up kissing once or twice – hot, passionate kisses that turned him inside out.

After the last time, they had promised each other that they would figure out the whole them-slash-Brad thing. But it had been a couple of days and he and Sienna hadn't spoken at all. Jason didn't know what that meant. Maybe it meant Sienna just wanted to pretend the kissing had never happened and stick with Brad. The trouble was that if Jason couldn't be with her soon – with no hiding and no pretending necessary – he felt he'd go mad.

'Am I wrong?' Dani asked.

'You're not wrong,' Jason said quietly. 'But, like I said, Sienna's with somebody else.' He felt relieved when Kristy bounded back over to them. He didn't want to discuss the Sienna situation with his sister.

'Hey, Kristy, don't you think Sienna and my brother would make a cute couple?' Dani asked.

Jason's mouth dropped open in shock. How could she just ask something so blatant? 'Danielle—' he began.

'Absolutely,' Kristy replied. 'Couples are all about the contrast. Sienna has black hair and almost black eyes.' She turned to Jason. 'And you're more young Heath Ledger-ish, all blond and blue eyes and everything. You two would look amazing together.'

'And that's all that matters,' Jason joked, trying to act as if this subject didn't bother him.

'No, but you guys have the vibe too,' Kristy added.

Did everyone see this thing that sparked between him and Sienna? Jason wondered. Did Brad?

'The vibe is more important really,' Kristy went on. 'The looks thing is just—'

'Madame Rosa's Palm Reading,' Jason said loudly, interrupting her. 'You guys have got to do that. Can't miss it.'

'Jason, this wasn't on the list we made,' Dani said as she followed him over to a blue and purple tent that had been set up between two of the booths.

'But look at it. It's the best thing here,' Jason answered. Anything to get them off the Sienna subject. 'And, hey, look, no line!' He ducked into the tent and saw the kind of psychic he'd expected to see all over the fair. She wore a long, gauzy skirt of white and gold, a white peasant blouse and a necklace made of small gold coins. There was no headscarf, but Jason could see gold hoop earrings glinting beneath Madame Rosa's wild gray curls.

'Vel-come,' she said.

Outstanding, Jason thought. *She's actually going for a Romanian accent. Well, good for her.* Jason would have had an easier time believing a psychic prediction from somebody in regular jeans and a T-shirt than from this lady right out of some old movie but, whatever, he was here for the distraction and Madame Rosa was certainly that.

'My sister wants to get her palm read,' Jason told Madame Rosa. 'I'll pay.'

'Can you tell who is going to ask her to the masked ball?' Kristy demanded as Madame Rosa took Dani's hand.

'Can you tell me if that note I found near my locker was for me or for someone else?' Dani asked.

'Oh, and you have to say if Max likes her or not. She keeps saying he doesn't, but I know he does,' Kristy added.

'Oh, thanks, Kristy,' Dani said. 'That's so gross.'

Operation Madame Rosa successful, Jason thought. Dani and Kristy were so interested in what the psychic had to say that they'd forgotten all about him and Sienna.

'Hush,' Madame Rosa said. 'I need to concentrate.' She stared down at Dani's palm for a long moment, then ran her finger over the deepest line that ran horizontally across the top of Dani's hand. 'This is your heart line. Do you see this star, here?'

Jason leaned forward and saw several short lines crossing the main line in a way that looked sort of like a star – in that way that little kids draw stars. 'A star means happiness in your marriage,' Madame Rosa continued.

'I better not be getting married soon,' Dani said. 'I'm planning to have some fun first. My Aunt Bianca might let me work in her casting agency.'

'Yeah, you need to be available for any of those hot actors that come in wanting to be discovered,' Kristy agreed.

'The marriage comes later,' Madame Rosa confirmed.

Jason had the feeling she was the kind of fortune-teller who made money by telling people exactly what they wanted to hear. People like Dani made it especially easy by spelling out exactly what Madame Rosa should, quote unquote, predict.

'But the star is also significant now,' the old lady was saying. 'Stars hold the key for you. Stars will lead you to your heart's desire. They will lead to your true love. Keep your eyes on the stars.' Madame Rosa released Dani's hand.

'Is that everything?' Kristy asked, echoing Jason's thoughts. He had read more substantial predictions in newspaper astrology columns.

'I tell people vat they need to know,' Madame Rosa said, tossing in a little accent again. 'Sometimes zat takes hours. Sometimes a few minutes. Your friend now knows everything she needs to in order to find the love she vants.'

'Will I find it soon?' Dani asked.

'As zoon as you begin to look in the right place,' Madame Rosa assured her.

Well, that's nice and specific, Jason thought as he reached for his wallet. At least Madame Rosa was cheap. The sign outside the tent had said five bucks. He handed her a ten, and waited for his change.

'There's zomething you should know,' she told him.

Of course there is. That way you can keep the whole ten, Jason thought.

'What is it?' Dani asked. She nudged Jason. 'I want to know.'

'Fine.' Jason held out his hand. The so-called psychic grabbed it and pulled it right up to her face. She spent about thirty seconds studying his palm in silence. Building up the suspense, Jason figured.

'Your love line is strong and deep. You will experience true love,' Madame Rosa announced.

'Si-en-na,' Dani and Kristy said together.

And we're back to that. So much for the distraction, Jason thought.

'This second line above your love line means that you have been helped by your loved one,' Madame Rosa continued.

That was actually true, Jason thought. Sienna had

helped him. When his best friend from Michigan, Tyler, had stolen a vampire artefact – not knowing it was a vampire artefact – Sienna had helped Jason save Tyler's life. And it had badly needed saving because the DeVere Heights Vampire Council had voted to kill him for what he'd done.

'She trusted you with her deepest secret,' Madame Rosa went on. 'So perhaps she loves you too, yes?'

Jason's eyebrows shot up. Sienna *had* trusted him with a big secret – the fact that she was a vampire. But Madame Rosa couldn't possibly know that. She was just making stuff up. Right?

'But vat I am most interested in vith you is your fate line.' Madame Rosa ran one long deep red fingernail up the line that started near the base of Jason's palm and ended about three-quarters of the way to his middle finger. 'You see this island where the line breaks?' She tapped the spot, and Jason nodded.

'That vorries me. You come to this point in your life soon. And it is a time of great danger for you. Your fate vill be decided von way or the other,' Madame Rosa continued.

'What's going to happen? You have to give him more than that!' Dani burst out, actually sounding anxious now.

'I cannot. That is all I see,' Madame Rosa said, tightening her grip on Jason's hand.

'Isn't there something you can do?' Kristy asked. 'A talisman you can give him to wear or something?'

Madame Rosa shook her head. 'He alone vill determine his fate.'

Now that surprised him. Jason had thought that for, say, fifty bucks, she'd offer him a lifetime of protection with a money-back guarantee – especially since he'd never see her again.

Madame Rosa locked eyes with Jason. 'The only varning I can give is to bevare of the cold. There is a connection there to the danger. So bevare of the cold!' As she spoke, a shiver seemed to run through her fingers and into Jason: a rush of ice that traveled up his arm and into his heart.

She knew about Sienna having a secret, he thought. Maybe she wasn't a complete fraud, after all.

He quickly pulled his hand away. 'Thanks. I'll, uh, keep that in mind,' he said, shoving himself hurriedly to his feet and leading the way out of the tent as the coldness of unease continued to course through his body.

TWO

An ice pick of cold stabbed into the back of Jason's left eye. 'Now I know what Madame Rosa's warning meant,' he gasped, shoving his mint-chip milkshake away.

'What?' Dani demanded.

'I shouldn't have sucked that down so fast. I've got a killer ice-cream headache now,' Jason explained, toying with the half-empty cup.

Dani and Kristy both shot him the Eyes Of Death.

'Kidding. Just kidding,' Jason said, and took another cautious sip of his shake. He and the girls had decided to make a stop at a 31 Flavors on the way home from the psychic fair. 'I completely respect Madame Rosa.' He gave the lump of ice cream in his shake a stir. 'Look, it's not that I don't believe that psychic ability exists,' he explained. 'But the fair just seemed more about raking in the big bucks.' He smiled at Dani. 'Something you will not be doing while taking care of my chores for the next four weeks, since you'll be handling them for free.'

'Yeah, yeah. But it's *three* weeks, not four,' Dani reminded him. 'And maybe some of the stuff at the fair was fake, but I don't think you should assume all of it was. I want you to be careful, like Madame Rosa told you to be.'

'But I already survived the ice-cream headache,' Jason told her. 'If it hadn't been for Rosa, I might have kept on drinking without a break and my eyeballs might have frozen!'

'Just be a little careful, idiot,' Dani insisted.

'What about you?' Kristy asked Dani. 'What do you think you should be doing? Madame Rosa told you to pay attention to the stars.' She popped the last little bite of her sugar cone into her mouth. And then an idea seemed to hit her. She chewed frantically, waving her hand in front of her face. 'Ooh! I got it!' she cried, as soon as she'd swallowed the cone. 'Maybe a movie star is going to take you to the masked ball!'

Jason knew Kristy was referring to the Christmas Charity Masked Ball being given by Sienna's parents. They gave the ball every year to raise money for home-less shelters in South Central, and had already booked Sandhurst Castle for this year's ball. Jason couldn't help wondering if he and Sienna would have worked out the them-slash-Brad issue by then.

'Well, there are a few sons of movie stars at our school,' Dani reminded Kristy. 'Oooh, maybe Madame Rosa meant Zach Lafrenière! He had that part in that movie that time. He's not exactly a star, but—'

'He will be,' Kristy said firmly. 'You can't look like Zach, ooze charisma like Zach, and not be a star. And I can so see you with him. He's never gone out with a sophomore before, but you weren't in town until this semester!'

'Maybe Madame Rosa meant you should pay more attention to zee 'oroscope,' Jason suggested. He so didn't want Dani going after Zach. Jason had nothing against the guy. Actually, he and Zach were . . . well, not friends, exactly, but they had an understanding.

Zach had come through in a big way when Tyler had stolen the vampire artefact from, oh yeah, Zach's house! The Vampire Council had been ready to kill Tyler. But Zach went against them – even though he was the newest and youngest member of the council – to help Jason and Sienna get Tyler out of Malibu and safely back to Michigan.

But helpful as Zach had been, he was also deep in the vampire world. He knew secrets that even Sienna didn't know. And that could end up being dangerous for Dani – especially since she had no idea that the

21

most popular kids at their school were *all* vampires. No idea that their own Aunt Bianca – who Dani wanted to work for someday – was on the Vampire High Council, an even more powerful organization than the DeVere Heights outfit. And no idea that vampires even existed. She'd been lecturing Jason about keeping an open mind all day, but Jason knew that not even the tiniest bit of her brain considered the possibility that vampires were real.

'I wonder if Mom knows the exact time of my birth,' Dani was saying.

'You'll need it to get a really accurate horoscope done,' Kristy replied.

The girls were completely wrapped up in a discussion of horoscopes now, Jason noted with relief. He wanted to keep it that way. Horoscopes were safer than vampires. Much safer.

Jason had planned to sleep well into the afternoon on Sunday to make up for the torment of getting up practically pre-dawn the day before to play chauffeur. But the first day of December was so sunny and warm that he was out of the house and trotting down the wooden steps to Surfrider Beach by eleven, his surfboard held over his head.

Maybe other people were used to December days that felt like June. But this Michigan boy wasn't, and he didn't plan to waste any of the sun.

Adam Turnball, who Dani always called Jason's wingman, followed him, carrying the only thing he planned to surf: a beach towel with a picture of Alfred Hitchcock on it. Alfred Hitchcock in swimming trunks. Not such a pretty sight. In his other hand, Adam carried his video camera.

'You sure you don't want to try surfing?' Jason asked Adam. 'We can rent you a board real quick, and I'll pass on all the wisdom I've learned from the Surf Rabbi.' Jason had been taking lessons for months from the fifty-something rabbi who'd ridden the waves all over the world.

'First, I'm going to fry my lily-white skin to a shade of tender pink,' Adam told him. 'Then I'm going to shoot some stuff on the beach. I want to experiment with color, the way Spielberg used red in *Schindler's List*, and I need some footage to—' He stopped abruptly and studied Jason for a moment. 'Your eyes have already started looking like donuts.'

'What?' Jason asked.

'You know, glazed. Try to keep up,' Adam explained. 'Now make the rabbi proud. Go do your Johnny Utah impression. See you later.' He made shooing motions until Jason turned and headed for the ocean.

Even though the day was so warm, Jason was glad he'd decided to wear his wetsuit as he jogged into the cold water. *Dani would probably tell me not to go in*, he thought. She was sure Madame Rosa was a true psychic, but Jason suspected that that was because Madame Rosa had told Dani she'd find love. Dani had been wanting a boyfriend since they'd moved here, but so far nobody had come up to her standards. She'd always been like that, refusing to go out with a guy unless he was perfect in every way – cute, popular, funny *and* smart. She should've asked Madame Rosa where to find a guy like that, Jason reflected.

Enough thinking about the psychic fair, he told himself. Giving up a whole Saturday to it was enough. Now he was going to recharge his primordial batteries, as the rabbi said. Jason wasn't sure exactly what that meant. But he did feel like surfing recharged *something*.

He slid onto his board and started to paddle out to the line-up, where all the surfers waited to pick their waves. Not too many surf dogs out today. Things got a little quieter on the beach post-summer.

Jason spotted a wave coming at him that was big enough to push him halfway back to shore. Time to duck-dive it. He kept the Surf Rabbi's instructions in mind as he stretched his hands out in front of him and pushed down the nose of his short board. Just before the wave broke, he took a deep breath and kept the pressure on the board until it submerged completely. When the wave passed, he angled the board up, resurfaced and kept paddling out.

He remembered how, when he'd first started taking lessons, just making it to the line-up had pretty much exhausted him. Now at least he'd gotten good enough that he still had some energy left to actually surf. He kept paddling and duck-diving until he was out far enough to take his place with the other surfers, then he pulled himself into a sitting position and stared out at the ocean, looking for the wave he wanted to ride.

He let a couple go by, then spotted the one he wanted. Jason used his hands and feet to turn the board so it was facing the beach. Then he pushed the board back, stretched out on top of it and started paddling. He felt the water swell underneath him, tensed for a moment, then snapped into the pop-up and rose to his feet.

I'm surfing, he couldn't help thinking. It still felt so completely cool. He was *surfing*. That's all he wanted to do all day: ride in, then paddle out, so he could ride back in again.

At least that's all he wanted to do until he hit the beach after ride five and saw Sienna, with a bunch of other people from school. They were setting up a volleyball net. And suddenly, all Jason wanted to do was play volleyball.

He headed over to Adam. 'Volleyball game starting up. Belle, Van Dyke, Brad . . .'

'Sienna,' Adam added.

'Wanna head over?' Jason asked, stripping off his wetsuit.

'I don't really do volleyball,' Adam answered, but he shoved himself to his feet. 'But I guess I can suffer through a game where hot girls jump up and down a lot, if it means so much to you.'

Jason toweled off, pulled shorts and a T-shirt over his bathing suit and ran his fingers through his hair. 'OK. Let's go. But with all that jumping up and down, don't get so distracted that you forget Belle has one insanely jealous boyfriend.'

'Ah, Dominic. Make that insanely jealous with extremely low impulse control,' Adam agreed as they headed across the sand. 'I will keep my eyes off Belle. Not that she makes it easy.'

True. Today Belle was dressed like Daisy Duke, except Daisy Duke never wore a diamond belly ring.

She'd even managed to wrangle her short blonde hair into pigtails.

'You guys playing?' Brad called.

'Yeah,' Jason called back, getting the usual hit of guilt he felt whenever he saw Brad. His eyes drifted to Sienna. When exactly was the whole sorting out of the them-slash-Brad situation going to happen? It wasn't cool to keep kissing each other behind Brad's back. They had to make some kind of decision. *The next time I see Sienna alone, I'm going to talk to her about it*, he decided. *We'll figure it out together.*

'You're both on Zach's team,' Brad told them.

'That leaves me with one more player,' Zach said, his eyes hidden by a pair of smoky Diesel sunglasses.

'Yeah, but you've also got Van Dyke, so it's all fair,' Brad joked. Brad and Van Dyke were always insulting each other in true best-friend style.

As Jason and Adam took their places on Zach's team, Jason noted that the non-vamps were now evenly divided. Brad had Kyle Priesmeyer and Aaron Harberts from the swim team. And Zach had Jason and Adam.

'Service!' Zach yelled. A second later, the ball went flying over the net. Sienna managed to hit it with one hand. It would have made it back over the net on its own, but Dominic gave it an assist from the front row.

He leaped up as the ball flew over his head, and spiked it. Sand flew up like a dry fountain when it hit right in front of Maggie Roy's toes.

Maggie leaned down to pick up the ball. Jason and Adam exchanged a glance. The thing had sunk about a foot in the sand.

'Holy crap,' Priesmeyer muttered. He ran both hands over his shaved head.

'You been taking more than the recommended dose of Liquid Mojo?' Brad asked.

'You wanna watch it. It can be dangerous,' Scott Challon added.

It wasn't that Jason knew so many of the vampires' secrets, but he knew enough to translate what Brad and Scott were telling Dominic. Hell, he could even translate it into Pig Latin. *Ixnay on the upersay engthstray.*

All the vampires were crazy strong, as well as crazy beautiful. They kept their looks toned down to movie-star gorgeous, and they usually kept their muscle power in check too. Dominic just wasn't good with the self-control – in any area. Jason had seen him almost annihilate a guy who was built like a meat freezer after the guy had hit on Belle.

'Good one, baby,' Belle called to Dominic as Maggie tossed the ball over the net.

'You're on our team,' Maggie reminded her.

'Oh. Whoops,' Belle said with a laugh. 'Go, us!'

'You can cheer for us if you want, Belle,' Erin Henry joked.

Sienna moved into the server position. It almost hurt to look at her. Her long black hair picked up sparks from the sun. And even in December, her skin was golden. Yeah, it almost hurt to look at her – especially when it was impossible to touch her.

Brad was nothing like Dominic in the jealousy department. If he had been, Jason would probably be dead by now. How could Brad miss the way Jason looked at his girlfriend? Hard as Jason tried not to stare, he—

Whomp! Sienna slammed the ball across the net, aiming right at Jason. He caught a glimpse of a playful smile on her face as the ball whizzed toward the sand at his feet.

Oh, no, Jason thought. *I'm not letting her get away with* that!

He dove for the ball, managing to get his clasped hands underneath it just before it hit the ground. He shot it up into the air and Scott tapped it easily back over the net.

Jason leaped back onto his feet in time to get the

next volley and they all played on until Adam somehow whacked the ball out of bounds on their own side of the net. As they changed positions, Jason shot a look at Sienna.

She was looking back, her dark eyes shining, and Jason felt a flush of pleasure. He hadn't made a complete fool of himself, then, even playing with all these superhero types. Sienna blushed, too, the tiniest bit.

She's thinking the same thing I am, Jason thought with complete certainty. *She's thinking that we should be together.*

'You're actually going jogging now? After the surfing and the volleyball?' Adam shook his head.

'I find my life easier to manage if I'm semi-exhausted at all times,' Jason told him. 'It lowers my stupidity level.'

'I think it works in the opposite direction,' Adam said. 'If you're tired, you're stupider. Look it up.'

'Not me,' Jason muttered. 'When I'm lacking energy, I'm less likely to do stupid things that I shouldn't do.' *Like kiss my friend's girlfriend,* he added silently.

Adam rubbed his arm. 'Well, I'm going to have to pull out the BenGay. I got a bruise from Belle. *Belle.* A petite little *girl!*'

'A petite little *vampire*,' Jason corrected him. 'You know they're super-strong.'

'Yeah, well, strong is one thing. But this is ridiculous – my shoulder got in the way of her hand when she was going for the ball. And now, BenGay. Maybe some Epsom Salts.'

'That's what happens when we mortals try to play with the superheroes,' Jason said. 'I wouldn't be surprised if I had some black and blue on me, too.'

'I doubt it. You're all sporty and impressive yourself,' Adam muttered good-naturedly as he gathered up his beach gear and camera. 'Anyway, I'm out. Got to do a weekend's worth of homework in one night.' He glanced up at the parking lot at the top of the cliffs. 'Not too many cars – and I use the word loosely, because I'm including my Vespa – left up there now.'

'I'm not going to stay much longer either,' Jason told him. 'See you in history.' Jason gave Adam a half salute and started to jog down the beach toward the pier. The sun would be beginning to set when he turned back and he could catch the view.

Not that the view going in this direction was bad – he hadn't managed to find a bad view in Malibu yet – and he had it mostly to himself. There were a few surfers still at the line-up. A golden retriever who wanted his ball thrown into the water again and again and again. The golden retriever's person who seemed happy to keep throwing. And a couple making out, mostly covered by their beach blanket.

By the time he decided to turn around, the only other human he could spot was one seal-like surfer out there in his wetsuit. That was one of the cool things about a winter's day in Malibu: sometimes it was like you had your own private island – as long as you didn't look over at the Pacific Coast Highway, running along the top of the cliffs.

The sun was an orange-red ball in a crimson sky that was deepening to purple. *Excessive.*

Jason veered toward his beach towel as a cool wind suddenly blew across the beach, making the hairs on his arms stand up. He shivered, feeling cold in the evening air. *Bevare the cold,* a little voice whispered in his head.

Jason ignored it. A cold wind in December was hardly something to worry about. He reached his beach towel and noted that his wetsuit was completely dry. He could just stuff it in his backpack. He leaned forward, bending his knees a little, to grab the pack—

Thunk! Jason felt something cold and hard slam into his body.

The impact forced him to stagger backwards. Red dots – like a dozen tiny setting suns – filled his vision for a moment. He blinked and looked down to see a thin metal bar sticking out of his chest. His stomach slowly turned over. Metal. In his body. His brain tried to understand.

The metal shone bright silver, reflecting the dying rays of the sun as Jason gently touched the silver shaft. Waves of cold pain radiated from the metal into every part of his body. *How did it get . . .? Did someone . . .?*

Jason realized that it didn't matter. He just needed to get out of there – fast!

He took one step before his knees buckled. The sand and the ocean and the red-orange sun all slid away into blackness.

THREE

'Jason. *Jason!*'

The voice came in a whisper. Or else the person speaking was very far away. Jason tried to open his eyes so he could tell which. He managed to crack them about an eighth of an inch. His eyelids felt like they'd been turned to lead.

'Jason, you *are* awake! I thought so.'

Dani. It was Dani's voice. Louder now. Jason struggled to open his eyes a little wider, and saw Dani's face, hazy-blurry, hovering above his own. 'Why're you . . . in my room?' he complained. 'I can sleep. Sunday.'

'Jase, you're in the hospital,' Dani said slowly.

It was like hearing the word 'hospital' brought the pain back. An intense throbbing, high on the left side of his chest, sliced through his fuzzy head and everything around him came into sharp focus: Dani's face, the plastic pitcher on the nightstand, the thin white sheets, the yellow curtain around his hospital bed. Hospital bed. He was in the freakin' *hospital*.

'This old surfer guy found you passed out on the beach,' Dani continued. 'If he hadn't been around . . .' She shook her head, not finishing the thought. 'Do you remember anything? I know the cops are going to want to talk to you.'

'Can I get . . .?' He flopped one hand toward the pitcher.

'Of course. Sure.' Dani seemed happy to have something to do. She leaped up, filled a glass with water, then held his head up enough for him to take a few sips. He felt like he'd been eating sand.

'Mom and Dad are trying to get here. All the flights out of Manhattan are snowed in. Mom's in a meltdown, of course,' Dani told him, putting the glass back down.

'S'OK. I'm fine,' Jason managed to get out.

'Yeah. That's what the doctor said,' Dani answered. 'She talked to Mom and Dad too. You got hit high enough in the chest that it didn't damage your heart or lungs or anything vital.' She sat down, then immediately stood back up again. 'Do you want anything else? Another pillow? Or Jell-o? Don't you always have to eat Jell-o in hospital?'

'You know I hate Jell-o,' Jason croaked, smiling at her, trying to calm her down.

'Well, *I* could eat it. I love the wiggly,' Dani said. She was trying to sound light, but Jason could see that her gray eyes were dark with worry. 'Do you remember any of what happened?' she asked again, getting serious.

Jason shook his head. Big mistake. He'd been hit in the chest, but something inside his skull felt like it had shattered. And the shaking just rattled all the pieces around.

'I remember jogging. The beach had emptied out. I was heading back toward the sunset. I remember starting to pick up my beach gear. Then something slammed into me and I felt cold.' Jason shrugged. Pain immediately exploded from the hot nugget in his chest. *Note to self: no shrugging and no head shaking.*

'Cold!' Dani's eyes widened. 'Jason, Madame Rosa was right! She said "beware the cold", remember?'

'I think the word was "bevare",' Jason answered. He yawned. He'd only been awake for a few minutes, but he felt exhausted. 'And what she should have told me to bevare of . . . was flying . . . pieces of . . . pointed metal.'

His eyelids closed. The bed seemed to lift off the floor and spin for a moment. He thought Dani was saying something, but she was sounding really far away again . . .

* * *

Jason slowly opened his eyes again. Plastic pitcher. Thin white sheets. Sienna's face. Yellow curtain. He was still in the hospital.

Back it up. *Sienna's* face? He blinked a few times. Yeah, it was Sienna sitting by his bed and not Dani.

'You're awake,' she said.

'People seem to feel the need to tell me that lately,' Jason commented. 'Since we're playing state-the-obvious, you're gorgeous.' He didn't think he'd ever said anything quite so blatant to her before. But he was in the hospital, which basically gave him a get-out-of-jail-free card. And she *was* gorgeous. Even if you made everything else about her ordinary and just kept the lips, all pink and plump, she'd be gorgeous.

'You're medicated, Michigan,' Sienna told him, but she smiled. With the lips.

'I do feel a little . . . woozy,' Jason admitted. 'Like, wasn't Dani here when I went to sleep?'

'Dani spent all of last night here,' Sienna told him. 'And half of today. I kicked her out. I told her she wasn't allowed back until she'd had at least five hours' sleep in her own bed.'

'Wait. You're saying it's, like, Monday afternoon?' Jason asked.

Sienna glanced at the watch on her slender wrist. 'Six-seventeen p.m. on Monday, December second.'

Jason used both hands to try and shove himself into a sitting position, ignoring the jolts of pain rocking his body. Sienna was at his side almost instantly. She had him propped up against two pillows effortlessly. It was so easy to forget how strong she was.

Especially when she was so close. Close enough that her tangy-sweet smell filled his nose. Close enough that her long, inky hair was brushing the skin of his bare arms.

'How did you even know I was here?' Jason said, because he had to say something.

Sienna smoothed the sheet gently over his chest and sat back down. 'A little thing called gossip. Haven't you figured out that the DeVere High grapevine's pretty efficient yet?'

'OK, well I need you to tell me everything you've heard about that Jason Freeman guy. Because all I know is I ended up with a piece of metal stuck in me. I don't even know how it got there. Did something blow up? Some kind of freak accident? I can't believe I didn't ask Dani any of this. My brain was kind of all over the place.'

'You've been in and out of consciousness,' Sienna

explained. 'Are you sure you're ready to hear everything right now?'

'More than ready.'

'Jason, you were shot with a crossbow. That piece of metal – it was a crossbow bolt.'

'Someone shot me?' His heart started to pound, and he could feel every beat in his wound. He took a long breath. 'OK, I guess my next question is, did this person mean to shoot me? Or were they just fooling around and aren't too handy with a crossbow?'

'They didn't stay and help you,' Sienna answered. 'So . . .'

'Yeah. And the whole beach was deserted. You'd have to have some accident to hit the only person out there.' A memory flashed through Jason's brain. He had bent down to get his backpack just before the arrow hit.

'Are you OK?' Sienna asked. 'You suddenly went pale.'

'I was just thinking . . . I bent down right before I was hit,' Jason explained. 'So the arrow should have gone lower.'

'Lower? But then . . . it would have gone right through your heart!' Sienna said in a trembling voice, her eyes suddenly bright with unshed tears. 'It would probably have killed you!'

'Yeah,' Jason agreed. It was all he could think of to say. The idea that he had come so close to death was almost impossible to take in.

Sienna did a little shimmy in her seat, as if to shake off the morbid thoughts. When she spoke again, her voice was steady. 'So, who do we know who would want you dead?' she asked, all business.

Jason knew the answer immediately: vampires. Vampires, because he knew their secret. Vampires, because Jason's friend had stolen one of their most valued relics – even though Jason had been the one to get it back.

'I don't have to ask what you're thinking now,' Sienna sighed, leaning back in her chair, away from him. 'You're thinking whoever did it has to be one of my kind.'

'Gorgeous girls?' Jason could practically hear the words fall flat. 'Sienna, I don't want to hurt you. We both know how much you've done for me, how much you've risked. And not just you, but Zach too. I don't look at all of your kind and think, *bad*. Or *good*.' He rubbed the bridge of his nose with his thumb. 'It's just that the only really big, intense stuff I've ever been involved in – the kind of stuff people get killed over – is stuff that also involves . . .' He let the sentence trail off. He wasn't going to use the word 'vampire' in the hospital where anyone could walk in. And Sienna knew what he meant.

'What about Adam?' Jason asked urgently, as a new thought struck him. 'He knows everything I do. And he helped me get Tyler away from the— From the Council. What if the same person is after him? Did you see Adam at school today? Where's my cell?' Jason scanned the room, looking for his backpack.

'You can't use cells in here,' Sienna said. 'And I saw Adam at school. I also saw him about an hour ago when he came by to visit you. He's fine, Jason.'

'For a second I thought he could be lying somewhere with a crossbow bolt through his heart,' Jason admitted.

'I know,' Sienna said. 'But think about it. Think about who really knows enough to possibly want to hurt you. Only Zach, Brad, and I know that you found out the truth about us. We also know that it was a friend of yours who stole from us, but you kept him from discovering the truth.'

'You're right.' Jason nodded. 'And if I can't trust you, Brad and Zach at this point, I can't trust anybody.' Brad and Sienna had never threatened him, never even seemed to dislike him, not even at the beginning.

They'd both been friendly, right from day one. Zach *had* definitely seemed like he'd rather not have Jason around, but not in a wanting-him-dead kind of way. In fact, Zach had saved Jason's life. And Jason had saved Zach's. They were cool with each other.

'I'm glad you've managed to remember that,' Sienna said. 'And today the three of us got together to talk about whether any of our special friends could have been involved. We went through every possibility and we're certain that the shooter wasn't one of us, Jason. Believe that.'

'I do.' He felt a little better just having talked it out with Sienna. 'I guess you guys wouldn't need anything like a crossbow anyway. A volleyball would be enough of a weapon.'

Sienna grinned. 'You know it.'

Sienna and Jason stared at each other for a long moment, then they both laughed, breaking the tension that always grew between them whenever they looked at each other for too long. Jason was relieved; his body wasn't exactly up to that kind of tension right now!

'Speaking of weapons, who walks around with a crossbow anyway?' Jason demanded. 'Think we're dealing with a wacko who wants to get a really great nickname in the papers?' He didn't think getting close to dead was actually funny. But if he had been shot by some passing nutcase, and not by a vampire out for vengeance, he had a much greater chance of staying alive for a while.

Sienna looked thoughtful. 'Using a crossbow isn't enough to get him the front page though. The guy needs more of an angle than that. He should get an agent,' she commented. 'So you want to hear what else is on the DeVere grapevine? You weren't the only topic today, you know.'

'Of course. Lay it on me,' Jason replied. He needed a distraction.

'Well, you were the top story. But Heaton West came a close second. Basically there was a poll of how many people thought she really wanted the "growth spurt" she had when she was away over Thanksgiving. And how many people thought her mother was the one who really wanted it.'

'Are you saying . . . ?'

Sienna raised an eyebrow. 'Tell me you didn't notice,' she challenged. 'We're talking more than a cup size here.'

Jason laughed and pain shot through his chest. He winced. 'Ow. You're not good for me. You make me laugh too much.'

'Then you really don't want to hear what Van Dyke got up to Saturday night,' Sienna said.

And pretty soon he was laughing again. About an hour later he realized that he'd basically been keeping Sienna hostage. 'You should take off. Go gather more gossip. Or create some,' he told her. 'I'm fine until Dani gets back.'

'No. I'll stay,' she said quickly. 'Unless you want to sleep or something and you'd feel weird with me here?'

'I want you to stay,' Jason said, thinking, *How could she not know that?* 'I just didn't want you to feel like you *had* to stay. To be polite or something.'

'I don't do many things just to be polite,' Sienna told him. 'I heard you were OK, but I had to see for myself,' she added in a rush.

Jason noticed that her voice had a slight tremor in it again. She was freaked. She was truly freaked by the idea that something could have happened to him.

'Thanks.' He reached out to squeeze her hand and reassure her, ignoring the protest from his chest wound.

Sienna slid her chair closer, its metal legs squeaking. And it was like the charge of the ions in the air shifted, the way they do after a thunderstorm. Everything felt newer, cleaner, *better*.

'Jason,' Sienna murmured, his name sounding like a term of endearment when she said it like that. 'If anything had happened to you . . .'

'It's OK,' he said, bringing her hand to his lips. 'I'm OK.'

Sienna leaned closer as he kissed her hand, her expression intense. 'We need to figure this out,' she said simply.

'I know,' Jason agreed. 'Because every time I see you, I want to kiss you.'

She nodded. 'Me too. Like now.'

She bent toward him, and the door swung open. Jason turned his head, expecting to see a nurse or a doctor coming to check up on him. But the person who stepped through the door wasn't a doctor or a nurse . . .

It was Brad.

FOUR

Brad's eyes flicked from Sienna to Jason, then back to Sienna.

It wasn't like he'd actually caught them kissing or anything, but it was a pretty intense moment and Brad wasn't stupid. Jason knew he had to sense it.

'Am I interrupting something?' Brad said finally, his tone cold and formal.

A wave of guilt washed over Jason. Brad had never been anything but great to him from day one. And how had Jason paid him back? By going after his girlfriend. *No.* That made it sound too calculating. By wanting Brad's girlfriend for his own – which was bad enough.

Neither Jason nor Sienna answered quickly enough for Brad. He turned and left.

Sienna stood up so fast she knocked over the flimsy plastic chair. She rushed after Brad. Without a word to Jason. Without even a *look*.

'What is your problem?' Jason heard Sienna say. He

could hear each word clearly, because she hadn't stopped to shut the door.

'Oh, sorry,' Brad snapped. 'I don't know what's the matter with me. It's just fine for my girlfriend to be staring at some other guy like she can't wait to jump into bed with him!'

Jason did not want to be hearing this, but a small part of him wanted to know what Sienna would say.

'That's ridiculous,' Sienna retorted. 'Jason's in hospital, Brad. I'm worried about him, OK? That's what you saw. You saw me looking like I cared about a friend of ours who almost died yesterday. Is that OK with you?'

She sounded ready to go up in flames. *Should I go out there? Roll my IV out into the hall and . . .* And do what? Jason didn't know exactly. It was hard to think of anything he could say that wouldn't be gasoline to the fire.

'Whatever! If you say so,' Brad told Sienna coldly. He sounded like he was trying to get a grip. 'Are you still coming over tonight?'

'I told Dani I'd stay here until she got back,' Sienna said. Jason could hear tension in her voice now, but not anger. She was trying to control herself too.

Jason could remind Sienna that he'd be fine by

himself. But he thought he'd let her make the call on her own.

'Do you have a problem with that?' Sienna asked, irritation creeping back into her voice.

'Did I say anything?' Brad demanded.

'No. You didn't have to,' Sienna shot back. 'I cancel one time to—'

'It's not one time,' Brad interrupted. 'You're always canceling. Or changing our plans into group things. It's like you don't want to be alone with me anymore.'

'Like the volleyball? I thought you had fun with everybody,' Sienna said.

'I would have had more fun spending the day at the beach alone with you,' Brad told her.

So the trouble between Sienna and Brad was bigger than this one incident. Jason didn't know how to feel about that. Part of him was glad. He didn't want to be solely responsible for their relationship issues.

'Brad, having time by ourselves is great, but—'

'Is this Jason Freeman's room?' a new voice interrupted.

'I'm taking off,' Brad said coldly. 'You stay with Jason as long as you want.'

A moment later, two men walked into Jason's room. One was forty-something, in a suit and tie, and looked kind of familiar. Jason squinted at him for a few seconds, trying to place him. Then it hit him. The guy was a detective. Detective Carson. Jason had talked to him after he'd found Carrie Smith's body. The detective had never figured out that Carrie had been killed by a rogue vampire. But why would he? Your basic sane Malibu P.D. official didn't believe in vampires.

'Raspberry-drizzled white-chocolate popcorn,' said the other guy, who was probably half Detective Carson's age, and had longish blond hair and stubble. He had picked up the bag of popcorn from Jason's nightstand and was giving it a shake. 'I like the fake butter myself. I wasn't raised right, I guess.'

'Actually, me too,' Jason agreed. 'I can go with cheese flavored. Especially if the cheese is actually cheez with a "z". But that's about it. My friend Adam must have left that when I was asleep. He likes weird movies and weird corn.'

'This is my partner—'

Before Detective Carson could finish, Sienna ducked into the room. 'I think I will go, if you're sure it's OK,' she said quietly to Jason.

'Sure. I'm fine,' Jason assured her. 'Thanks for coming.'

Sienna nodded, picked up her purse, and quickly slipped back out again.

'Nice,' the scruffy guy said, dropping into one of the chairs and glancing after Sienna.

Nice, as in nice girl who stopped by to visit hurt friend? Jason wondered. *Or nice, as in something Scruffy Guy shouldn't really be thinking about Sienna?*

'Like I was saying, this is my partner, Detective Tamburo,' Carson said, nodding toward Scruffy. 'I'm Detective Carson. We met—'

'After Carrie Smith died. Yeah. I remember,' Jason said.

'You're not too lucky, are you, sport?' Tamburo asked.

He needs to wear a nametag or something to say he's a detective, Jason thought. Carson looked the part, pretty much, with his suit and lace-up shoes. But Tamburo had on motorcycle boots, jeans that looked *real* distressed, not two-hundred-dollar-new distressed, and a black shirt that was unbuttoned too far for someone who had a day job that wasn't bartending.

'I guess I'm either not too lucky or incredibly lucky,' Jason answered. He touched the bandaged spot on his chest lightly. 'A little unluckier, and I wouldn't be alive. But a little luckier, and I'd be doing something a lot more fun right now!'

'With the babe?' Tamburo asked, one corner of his mouth tilting up in a lopsided grin.

'Or with one of my other friends,' Jason replied coolly, wondering how it was any of Tamburo's business.

Carson sat down in the other visitor chair. 'What can you tell us about what happened, Jason?'

Jason walked them through it. His decision to take a jog after his friends left. What he saw on the way out: the dog and its owner, the couple under the blanket, the surfers. What he saw on the way back: just the one surfer. Then bending down to get his wetsuit. The pain. The blackness.

'Our shooter is quite a marksman,' Carson remarked. 'If you hadn't leaned down, the bolt would have hit you square in the heart.'

'Thanks for reminding me,' Jason joked weakly.

'And you didn't get anything on him or her?' Carson asked.

'Even a general impression of height or weight? Anything?' Tamburo added, leaning forward, waiting for Jason's answer.

'The sun was right in my face. I didn't see anyone else on the beach,' Jason answered.

Carson let out a frustrated sigh. 'Could be this was a

random attack,' he said. 'But let's assume for a minute that it wasn't. Who would want to see you dead?'

'No one,' Jason replied immediately.

'Slow down,' Carson suggested. 'Take a little time and think about it. You never know what will motivate some people. Don't try to think of some huge reason. Just consider whether you've had any arguments with anyone lately. That kind of thing.'

'I haven't . . . There's nothing,' Jason said after he'd thought about it for a few minutes.

'What about Mr All-American?' Tamburo asked. 'We could hear him and the babe "talking" from down at the nurse's station. Didn't sound like he was a big fan of yours, my friend.'

'Brad?' Jason shook his head, starting up a headache to add to the pain in his chest. 'No way. Brad's, like, the nicest guy in school.'

'Yeah, right. Nicest guy in school yelling at his girl-friend for wanting to—'

Jason didn't let Tamburo finish. 'OK, yeah, Brad was pissed. He thought Sienna and I were, I don't know – having a moment? – when he walked in. They were arguing about that in the hall, but other stuff too. Stuff that had nothing to do with me. She doesn't spend enough time with him or whatever.'

Carson and Tamburo exchanged a look that Jason couldn't read. 'Brad and I are friends, OK? We're on the swim team together. I go to parties at his house,' Jason explained.

'OK,' Carson said. 'Let's move on. Was anything stolen when you were shot?'

'I hadn't even thought about that. I don't know what happened to my board. Or my car. I had my keys in my pocket. Whoever shot me could have grabbed them when I was out,' Jason answered.

'Your car and board were both still at the beach. Anything else?' Carson asked.

'My wallet, I guess.' Jason looked around the room. 'I'm not even sure where it would be. I don't even know where my clothes are.'

'As a detective, I would say . . .' Tamburo got up and opened the tiny closet across from Jason's bed. 'Yep. Clothes' – he quickly went through the pockets – 'but no wallet.'

Carson used the phone on the night stand to call the nurse's station. He asked if the wallet was in the bag with Jason's personal effects.

'Cell phone. Keys. Watch. No wallet,' Carson announced as he hung up the phone. 'What was in it?'

Before Jason could answer, Tamburo tapped his

collar bone. 'Nice bruise. Where'd you get it? Got one on your arm too.'

For a second, Jason couldn't remember. 'Maybe when I fell . . .' he began. Then he remembered. 'No, wait. It was playing volleyball.'

'Who were you playing with, King Kong?' Tamburo asked.

'And Godzilla,' Jason agreed. It was practically true. Vampires with super-strength could probably take on those two.

'What was in the wallet?' Carson asked again.

'Some cash – about sixty dollars,' Jason told him. 'An AmEx.'

Tamburo snorted, but didn't comment.

'And just, you know, wallet stuff: receipts, ticket stubs.' *Like the ones for the psychic fair*, Jason thought. But he did not feel the need to tell the detectives that he went to that particular event. 'A grocery list my mom gave me, maybe.'

Add to that a list of potential vampires he and Adam had come up with when they first figured out that there were actually vampires at DeVere High – but the detectives didn't need to know about that, either.

Carson frowned. 'I can't see you getting shot by a

crossbow for sixty dollars and a credit card. Remember to call and cancel it, by the way.'

'Seems like you just happened to get yourself in the path of a whack job with a lethal weapon,' Tamburo told Jason. 'I'm thinkin' our sicko isn't going to be happy until he's managed to off somebody with his little toy.' He turned his eyes – blue laser beams – on Jason. 'You sure you don't remember anything that can help us catch this freak before that happens?'

'I wish I did,' Jason answered.

Carson handed him a couple of business cards. 'This is where you can reach us if you remember anything later. I want you to call if you remember the slightest little thing – even a seagull flying by and pooping – OK?'

'Yeah. I will. I definitely will,' Jason promised. He didn't want his family, Sienna, or *anybody* walking around Malibu with a deranged crossbow-wielding killer on the loose.

FIVE

'You're awake!' Jason's mother exclaimed as she rushed into his hospital room, followed by Jason's dad and Dani.

Jason glanced at the clock over the door, trying to figure out just how long he'd been asleep. He was finding it hard to keep track of time here, but he thought it had probably been about two hours since the detectives had left.

'I'm going to have the words "Yep, I'm awake" tattooed on my forehead,' he answered, trying not to wince as his mom hugged him carefully.

'I'm sorry it took us so long to get here,' she told him as she gently let him go. 'I called and called, but you were always asleep, and I didn't want anyone to wake you.'

'I'm fine, Mom,' he told her.

'You're going to have to have that tattooed some-place too,' Jason's dad said, elbowing his wife out of the way and giving Jason a hug that brought tears of pain to his eyes. 'Your mother's going to have to hear that a dozen times a day for a month. Then she might believe it.'

'Doubtful,' Dani commented, perching on the windowsill. 'Try a dozen times a day for a *year*.'

'Your father was just as worried as I was,' Mrs Freeman replied. 'You should have heard him yell at those airline people. As if it was their fault we got snowed in.'

'I got Detective Carson on the phone before we took off,' Mr Freeman told Jason. 'He said he was coming by to talk to you.'

'Yeah, he and his partner were here a couple of hours ago. I couldn't tell them much though,' Jason answered.

His father frowned. 'I expect them to have some things to tell *us* pretty fast.'

There was a light tap on the door and Jason's doctor walked in. 'Ah, the whole family's here,' she said pleasantly, pushing her wire-rimmed glasses up into her reddish hair. 'I'm Dr Quazi. I've been treating Jason since they brought him in.'

Jason's mother pounced. 'How is he?'

'He's fine,' Dr Quazi answered. Jason shot his mom

a told-you-so smile. 'As I said on the phone, he was very fortunate in the location of the wound. None of his organs were touched.'

'Thank God,' Mrs Freeman said.

Dr Quazi put her glasses back on and studied Jason's chart. 'The pain and shock had him in and out of consciousness initially, but the wound itself should heal nicely,' she told them. 'Jason will need to keep it dry until the stitches come out, and he'll need to limit his activity for a while. I've told him no swimming for two months.'

'Are you listening to this, Jason? No swim team until the beginning of February,' his mother cautioned.

'And if there is any new swelling around the wound, or redness or drainage, or an increase in the skin temperature, please call me,' Dr Quazi concluded.

'So you're saying I can go home now? Right?' Jason asked.

Dr Quazi smiled. 'Right. After your parents fill out several dozen forms,' she answered. 'Please don't hesitate to call me if you have any questions or problems though.' She handed Jason her card and left the room, after being thanked a couple of times by Jason and his dad, once by Dani, and about fifty times by Jason's mom. Jason set the card on the nightstand along with Carson's and Tamburo's. He was going to need a new wallet before he left the building, the way he was collecting business cards.

'I'll go and handle the paperwork,' Mr Freeman announced. 'I know your mother won't want to let you out of her sight.'

Mrs Freeman sat down in the closest visitor's chair. It did seem like she planned to get some staring time in.

'Uh, how was New York?' Jason asked her.

She used both hands to push her hair away from her face. 'Do you know, it feels like about a hundred years since I've been anywhere but the airport trying to get back here?' she told him. She reached for her purse and stood up. 'I bet you a hundred dollars your father doesn't have his insurance cards with him. I'll take mine down and come right back.' She hurried to the doorway, then turned back and looked at Jason again. 'It's really good to see you safe,' she told him. Then she hurried off.

'I'm glad she's gone for a minute,' Dani said. 'I didn't want her to hear this. She's already freaked enough.'

Jason sat up a little straighter, trying to ignore the electric zaps in his chest. 'What?'

'Everybody's looking for Dominic Ames. He's

been missing since Sunday afternoon,' Dani told him.

'Sienna didn't say anything,' Jason said, frowning. He was sure she would have known. The vampire grapevine was way faster than the ordinary school one.

'It took everyone a while to figure it out,' Dani explained. 'Seems like Dominic's parents were out late on Sunday night, and they didn't even realize he hadn't come home. Then at school, nobody thought it was strange that he missed a day. He's kind of a class optional kind of guy anyway, right?'

'He shows up just enough to get by,' Jason agreed.

'So what I heard is that Belle went over to his place after school. Dominic wasn't there, but his mom was. She checked with the housekeeper, and it turns out Dominic hadn't slept in his bed Sunday night. I guess he's bed-making optional too. Anyway, his parents are calling everyone he knows. They've called the cops already.'

'Are the cops doing much? He hasn't been gone that long in cop time,' Jason said.

'Are you kidding? There's a big search happening,' Dani answered.

'Oh, right, I always forget how rich everyone in DeVere Heights is. I guess if someone from the Heights calls the police, they move, huh?' Jason observed.

'That's not it,' Dani told him. 'Or maybe it is, partly.' She leaned closer. 'But don't you get it, Jason? It's because of what happened to you.' Jason's wound gave an extra strong zap. 'Everyone's really scared that Dominic's missing and the guy who shot you with the crossbow is still out there somewhere!'

Jason flipped through the channels – again. Daytime TV sucked. He should have gone to school.

Yeah, because school is so much more amusing, he thought, settling on a rerun of the *Drew Carey Show* he'd already seen a couple of times.

'Do you want an apple, Jason?' his mother called from the kitchen. 'You should see how red and shiny they are.'

'No thanks,' Jason answered from the living room, trying not to let his impatience show in his voice. His mom turned into a demented, hyper-cheerful kindergarten teacher whenever he or Dani got hurt or sick. She'd just told him how red and shiny an apple was, for God's sake! And all day, she'd been trying to get him to eat stuff. Or trying to find out if he was too hot or too cold. Or trying to check his wound for symptoms of gangrene, or the flesh-eating super-virus, or whatever.

Yeah, school might have a low amusement value.

But it also had a lower annoyance value than home right now. There was no mom at school.

And there was Sienna.

Jason had been thinking about her all day. With day-time TV being so bad, his mind kept drifting to what had happened at the hospital. He wondered what she'd done after she left. Had she caught up to Brad? Had they had another fight? Had they made up?

At school, he'd have been able to suss things out. Get a vibe from Sienna just by sitting in class with her.

Jason picked up the remote again. He needed something to distract him. He'd already gone over every permutation of the situation between him, Sienna and Brad multiple times. His brains would start to leak out his ears if he kept it up.

Click. Soap opera. That wouldn't do it. Click. *Dr Phil*. Jason probably needed the guy, but no. Click. One of those home makeover shows. Click. *Teletubbies*.

The doorbell rang.

'I got it,' Jason yelled, abandoning the television.

'You're supposed to stay still,' his mother called.

'No one said motionless,' he answered. He pulled open the door and saw Adam standing there with a bag of what he hoped and suspected were cheese fries in one hand, and some DVDs in the other.

'At least one of those had better be an action . . .' Jason began, but he let his voice tail off because Adam wasn't talking, he wasn't already munching on whatever food was in the bag, and he wasn't smiling.

'What's going on?' Jason demanded.

'My dad just called on my cell,' Adam answered. 'Dominic's dead.'

SIX

'You could have been killed,' Mr Freeman said to Jason, shaking his head anxiously. 'A boy was shot through the heart with a crossbow bolt only about two hours after the attack on you. Clearly that monster wasn't going to be satisfied until somebody was dead. It could have been you.'

'Stop saying that,' Jason's mother begged. 'It's not . . . it's not dinner-table conversation.'

Like that's what's really bothering her, Jason thought. *Like she looks ready to cry for the second time in two days because our table manners are bad.*

Dani didn't look close to tears. She did look close to puking, but she hadn't really eaten enough to vomit. Jason hadn't been able to eat much either. Dominic was dead. Just the other day the guy had been playing volleyball – and now he was dead.

'Sorry,' Adam told Mrs Freeman. 'My dad talks about stuff like this constantly, whatever he's doing:

eating, mowing the lawn, probably in his sleep. It's a side-effect of being Chief of Police.'

'Don't apologize. We need to know this,' Mr Freeman said. 'Did your father give you any feeling about how close they are to catching the guy? What kind of evidence they've got? Anything like that?'

'He mostly keeps that stuff to himself,' Adam answered. 'But I know they found the body at that car detailing place over on Center. Right now, Dad's got all his people going over every inch of the place. Plus, they're searching the trunk of the El Camino where they found the body.'

Jason noticed a little shudder go through Dani at the word 'body'. His little sister was having a really hard time with this.

'Are the same detectives working on Dominic's case?' Jason asked Adam, hoping to feed Dani some sort of comforting info. 'Those guys seemed pretty sharp.'

'Yep. And they are sharp,' Adam confirmed, taking a big bite of chicken. 'Carson's been a detective for more than twenty years. And Tamburo's a real hotshot. He just transferred in from Vegas. They called him Tamburo the Terminator down there. That's how good he is at putting people away.'

'That's something,' Mr Freeman said.

'You should be expecting another conversation with Carson or Tamburo soon, by the way,' Adam informed Jason.

'I already told them everything I remember,' Jason protested.

'But now what you remember could help them find Dominic's murderer,' Adam pointed out, serving himself some more green beans – at least someone was up for eating. 'Unless there were two maniacs with crossbows running around Malibu on Sunday. But that would be movie reality. Not reality reality. Right, Dani?'

Adam must have noticed how freaked Dani was. He probably thought that including her in the conversation would make her feel better.

Dani managed a small smile. 'Yeah, and one maniac is definitely enough,' she answered.

'I hope the police are planning to put some safety measures in place until they do find the person who did this,' Jason's mother added. 'It wasn't long ago that that other girl from your school died. Karen Smith.'

'Carrie,' Adam corrected. He would know. He and Carrie had been kind of on the way to getting something going before she had been killed by a rogue vampire.

'At least we know for sure that that had nothing to do with this,' Jason's dad said. 'That was just a horrible accident.'

Jason shot Adam a look. The truth was, Carrie hadn't drowned. She'd been murdered by a vampire who had got caught up in a kind of vampire madness, called bloodlust.

'I think I'm done,' Dani said suddenly. 'Can I be excused? I think I want to go watch *Mean Girls* or something.'

Jason knew that *Mean Girls* was Dani's comfort movie. And so did his mom and dad. Jason saw them exchange a worried look.

Then Mrs Freeman stood up. 'I'll go with you. I wouldn't mind seeing it again,' she said brightly.

'Me too,' Mr Freeman said. 'I don't think I've ever managed to stay awake for the ending.' He followed Dani and Mrs Freeman out of the room.

'You've really heard this Tamburo guy is good?' Jason asked Adam when they were alone.

'Yeah. I mean, he's got a wild streak, as my father would put it,' Adam replied. 'I'd say he's fifty per cent Tommy Lee Jones in *The Fugitive*. Think the "check every dog house, hen house and outhouse" scene. Forty per cent Russell Crowe in *L.A. Confidential*.

And ten per cent Brad Pitt in *Thelma and Louise*.'

'As usual I need a translation, Mr Moviefone,' Jason complained. Adam was always referencing movies that no living person had seen. 'For starters, I thought Brad Pitt was a thief in *Thelma and Louise*.'

'Well, yeah, if you want to be all literal about it. Anyway, the point is Tamburo's thorough and tenacious. He follows his own rules and he's got attitude but he also has a sense of humor and, I guess you'd call it an honor code,' Adam explained.

'I guess we can trust him to get this thing solved then,' Jason said, standing up and stretching gingerly. His whole body still ached from the crossbow wound. 'My mom got some Bubbie's mochi to celebrate me being alive and everything,' he went on. 'I couldn't tell her that I'd rather have regular mint chip or something like that. I mean, rice paste around ice cream balls? What's with that? I'll tell you what: a way to damage some perfectly good ice cream, that's what.' He shook his head. 'Anyway, you want some?'

'Lead me to it, brother,' Adam said. 'I don't know how they even let you live in the Heights,' he added as he followed Jason into the kitchen. 'Don't you know Bubbie's mochi is *the* ice cream served at Nobu? You used to only be able to get it in Hawaii.'

'How do you even know that?' Jason countered. 'You're the son of the poor-but-honest Chief of Police, as you're always reminding me. So, what flavor you want? Papaya? Lychee? Green tea?'

'Surprise me,' Adam answered. 'This may be the only time I get my mouth around anything Bubbie's. As I am the son of the etcetera etcetera.'

Jason laughed as he opened the freezer. 'Mom does know me. There's a carton of mint chip in here too.' He suddenly felt a little hungry. 'You'll have to scoop it for me, because I'm wounded and all. The mochi's already in balls.'

'So I have a question for you,' Adam said.

'The ice-cream scooper's in the drawer next to the sink,' Jason answered.

'Funny.' Adam grabbed the scooper while Jason got down a couple of bowls from the cupboard, trying not to wince. The motion still made the hole in his chest angry. 'My question is, what's the connection between you and Dominic? You go to the same school, you both live in the Heights. What else?'

'We hang out with the same people sometimes. We've been seen at some of the same parties,' Jason answered automatically as Adam started dishing out the ice cream. Then he got it. 'Wait. You think Dominic and I were specifically targeted?. You don't think the crossbow killer just shot us because we happened to be in the wrong place at the wrong time?'

Adam shrugged. 'Maybe it was random. *Probably* was.'

Jason grabbed spoons. 'Want to take the ice cream out by the pool?' he asked. He knew it would be chilly out there. The temperature always dropped dramatically at night, no matter how warm it was during the day. But Jason had a little cabin fever.

'It's your party.'

Jason flicked on the backyard lights, and the pool light on the way outside. Then he stretched out on one of the lounge chairs. Adam took the one next to him.

'So we've established you and Dominic do have some things in common,' Adam persisted, digging into his first mochi ball. 'I mean, you're not a jealous asshole like Dominic, so people like you a little bit more . . .' He frowned. 'I guess I'm the asshole for talking about Dominic like that. I forgot he was dead for a second.'

'Yeah. It's hard to believe,' Jason agreed grimly. 'And even though the guy's dead, it's still true he was a bit of a jackass. But he was a small-time jackass. You have to be big-time to have somebody want to come after you with a crossbow, don't you?'

'Or you have to be a vampire,' Adam answered.

'Did I go unconscious for a minute?' Jason asked. 'Because I definitely missed something. What are you talking about?'

'When I was first doing all my vampire research, I read this article on the web about how in Medieval Europe vampire hunters used crossbows,' Adam explained.

Jason closed his eyes for a moment, then opened them and looked at Adam. 'Right away, I see three problems with this new theory of yours.'

'Hit me,' Adam said, slapping his chest with one hand, while eating his ice cream with the other.

'OK. One, we're thousands of miles from Europe. Two, we're hundreds of years on from Medieval times. And three – and pay attention because this is the big one – Dominic was a vampire, but, in case you haven't noticed, *I'm not*!'

Adam laughed. 'Good points. All of them.' The grin slid off his face. 'But I want you to keep thinking about possible connections between you and Dominic. If you're a target, we need to know about it, because we need to be prepared in case that maniac makes another run at you.'

'Fine. But I still say it's random,' Jason answered.

'Dominic and I don't have anything in common that someone would be willing to kill for.'

A breeze from the ocean rattled the palm fronds of the huge trees at the far end of the backyard, and gooseflesh rose on Jason's arms. He had the sudden urge to look over his shoulder to see if someone was watching him, but he refused to give in to his burst of paranoia.

Because it was just paranoia. Right?

When Jason walked across the high-school parking lot on Wednesday morning with Dani, he was still fighting off the creepy sensation that he was being watched. It didn't help that the whole school felt . . . eerie, somehow. People were standing around in the parking lot as if they didn't want to leave the relative safety of their cars. The usual before-school buzz of conversation was subdued, and most of the students looked tense and anxious. Obviously everybody was freaked out by Dominic's death.

But it was more than that, Jason realized. The reason he felt he was being watched was that he *was* being watched. He was getting a lot of curious looks from pretty much everyone else heading into the school.

'Yo, Freeman,' Harberts called as Jason and Dani

entered the main courtyard. 'You're back. Are you supposed to be back?'

'I missed you too much to stay away,' Jason joked. Technically, he was supposed to be home taking it easy for a few more days, but he'd managed to convince his parents that he'd be OK sitting around at school.

'I always knew you loved me,' Harberts responded. 'You going to come to practice? We're having a team meeting.'

'Yeah, I'll be there. I can't swim, but I'm still on the team, right?' Jason answered.

Harberts nodded and disappeared through one of the arches leading into the walkway around the main building.

'There's Billy,' Dani said. 'I need to ask him something. See you after.' She gave him a little wave and veered off toward her friend.

Erin fell into step beside him, taking Dani's place. 'I was just reading this article that said undereye circles are the look of choice for the spring runway. You're now completely fashion forward, just so you know.'

Jason rolled his eyes. 'That's what I've been striving for.'

'Seriously, are you OK?'

'I'm fine.' Jason figured he'd be saying that a lot

today. 'The bolt didn't hit anything vital. The wound'll take a little while to heal, but that's it.'

'Good. That's good. We were all worried about you.' They walked through the arch and into the dim walk-way beyond. 'I have to go by my locker. You know we're all supposed to go to the auditorium instead of home room, right?'

'Dani told me.' He took about three steps by himself before Adam caught up to him. Jason definitely wasn't going to have to worry about being lonely today.

'Your dad have any more info about Dominic's killer?' Jason asked.

'Nope. Dominic's body was clean. The car and trunk too,' Adam answered. 'Whoever stuffed him in there was very careful. They didn't leave anything behind. And it's not like Malibu doesn't have the money for all the best forensic toys. Believe me, anything that could be tested, scanned, or run through a centrifuge has been. It's like all three *CSI* shows rolled into one.'

'My father's not an idiot or anything, but I think he actually believes the world should work like it does on *CSI*,' Jason replied. 'He's going to expect, I don't know, your dad to uncover a grasshopper egg and a piece of thread and have the shooter locked away—'

'By the end of the hour?' Adam interrupted as they walked into the auditorium.

'He knows we aren't *actually* living in a TV show,' Jason responded. 'I figure your dad's probably got a few days, maybe a week.'

'Before what?' Adam asked.

Jason shrugged. 'Before he starts organizing parents' meetings or civilian task forces or something. He's a results-oriented kind of guy.' He dropped into a seat near the back of the room. The topic of the special assembly hadn't been announced, but he was sure it would be about Dominic. And Jason just didn't want an up-close-and-personal view of it all.

'Hey, you didn't by any chance come up with any other similarities between you and Dominic, did you?' Adam asked.

Jason was about to tell Adam that he really didn't want to talk about that now – and maybe not ever – when Principal Ito stepped out onto the stage.

'Welcome, everyone,' he said. 'We are here together on a sad day. As I think most of you know, one of our students, Dominic Ames, is no longer with us. Dominic was killed. Murdered. It's hard to understand. And even harder to accept. We're going to have grief counselors talk to you in smaller groups later in the day. We want you to have a time and place to express your feelings about Dominic and his death.'

Principal Ito lowered his head briefly. 'But first, we need to take a few moments to consider your safety. The person who murdered Dominic has not been apprehended. It is very likely he – or she – has attacked another student.' Heads all over the large room turned toward Jason, then back toward the principal. 'That's why we have two detectives with us today,' he continued. 'Detective Carson and Detective Tamburo. They will be outlining the safety procedures I expect every one of you to follow until further notice. Some of these apply while you're at school, others are town-wide regulations put into place by our Chief of Police, Sheriff Turnball.' A few heads swiveled toward Adam, who pretended not to notice. 'So now I'm going to turn things over to the detectives,' Principal Ito said. 'I expect you all to give them your full attention.'

There was an expectant hush as Carson walked up and took Principal Ito's place in front of the microphone. Tamburo climbed up on stage too, but he stayed off to one side, leaning one shoulder against the wall. His eyes roved over the crowd, his face expressionless.

'I wouldn't mind Motorcycle Boots arresting me,' a

girl – Jason thought she was a freshman – murmured nearby.

'God, Ariel,' someone else whispered. 'Inappropriate, much? Somebody died!'

'OK, this is going to be simple,' Carson announced. 'Until further notice, we need you all to stay on campus during school hours unless you have a pass from the office. Yes, that includes lunch,' he added as several hands went up. 'And I've been in your cafeteria, so you're not going to get me feeling sorry for you.

'We're also going to post a guard at the entrance to the parking lot. You all have a school ID, and you're all going to have to show it – students, teachers, support staff, everybody. That means you'll have to get here early tomorrow morning because there's going to be a line to get in,' Carson continued. There were mutters from his listeners.

This is going to make a lot of parents happy at least, Jason thought. *Including mine.* He wasn't exactly bummed to hear about it himself.

'Lastly, we're going to have a curfew for everyone under eighteen,' Carson told the group. 'You'll need to be home by nine p.m. I don't want to see any of you out on the streets after that time.' That one got a lot more mutters and some groans. 'Any questions?'

A few hands went up. Carson pointed to Kristy. Jason could only imagine what was going to come out of her mouth.

'What about the Christmas Charity Masked Ball? The one the Devereuxs give?' Kristy asked. 'Everyone's already bought their tickets and everything. And it goes on past nine.'

Carson shot a glance at Tamburo.

'It's a tough question for him,' Adam muttered. 'It's hard for even the P.D. to go up against charity *and* the Devereuxs. They give a lot to the Policeman's Ball too.'

'We have some time on that one,' Carson said at last. 'Hopefully, it won't even be an issue. If it is, we'll make an announcement later. Anything else?'

No hands went up.

'All right. That's it,' Carson said. 'Detective Tamburo and I will be pulling students out of class throughout the day. Some of you could have information you don't even realize is important that could help us find Dominic's killer. We want to thank you in advance for cooperating.' He gave a quick nod and stepped away from the mic.

Principal Ito moved back to the front of the stage. 'I'd like to end with a minute's silence for Dominic Ames.' He bowed his head.

Jason lowered his head too. He was ultra conscious

of the heat in his chest wound as he thought about Dominic. The silence in the room was so perfect that he could hear his own heart beating.

Then a small sound broke it. A small sniffling sound. Someone was crying.

The soft sounds turned into sobs, the choking kind, where you can hear that the person can hardly breathe. A moment later, Jason heard footsteps rushing up the center aisle. He looked up and saw Principal Ito hurrying Belle out of the auditorium. Her face was twisted with grief. She looked nothing like the playful, happy girl Jason knew.

With the principal gone, no one knew exactly when the silence should end. Eventually, hesitantly, people began to gather up their books and backpacks. Adam looked at Jason, shrugged, and stood up.

'Jason, wow, I just kept thinking how it could have been you who died!' Sukie Goodman from his chem class said as she walked by.

Before Jason could answer her, Brad moved up next to him.

'Yeah, it could have been you,' he said flatly. And Jason saw something cold and hard in Brad's eyes. Something that told him Brad wished it *had* been Jason.

SEVEN

Jason half wanted to ask Adam if he'd seen the look Brad gave him back in the auditorium. But then he figured it was probably better not to make a fuss about it. He hoped that whatever was eating Brad – could it still be a hangover from the argument with Sienna in the hospital? – would soon blow over.

'See you on the flip side,' Adam said when they parted ways at the end of the hall.

'If by that you mean history, then, yeah,' Jason answered.

As he headed toward calc, he spotted Maggie Roy, Van Dyke and Zach in an intense discussion near one of the trophy cases. Talking about Dominic, he assumed.

'Hey,' he called, slowing down as he got close to them.

None of them answered. They all just looked at him. Like they were thinking, *Who the hell are you and why are you talking to us?*

Which was halfway to normal for Zach. He was a loner, even within the vampire clique, and he didn't have a whole lot of time for humans. He didn't seem to dislike them or anything; he just didn't bother with them much. Kind of the way seniors didn't bother with freshmen. He and Jason had actually had a conversation or two, what with the mutual lifesaving and all, but they weren't exactly best friends. Still, the others weren't usually so standoffish.

Jason didn't know Maggie all that well. But they'd talked. They'd hung out at parties a little. Joked around some. Hell, they'd played volleyball on Sunday. As far as he knew, she'd never had a problem with him.

And Van Dyke. Van Dyke swam relay with him on the team. He and Jason were solid mid-level friends.

So what was the deal?

Jason hadn't expected a parade for being back in school. But he did think one of them would cough up the usual 'How are you?' to which Jason would respond with the usual 'Fine, thanks' before going on his way.

You need to get a grip, he told himself as he passed the three of them. *They're crushed by Dominic's death and you're bent out of shape because they didn't say 'hi'. Come on, Freeman!*

He stopped off at his locker to get his calc book. He

was going to have to make a locker stop between every class, since his injury wouldn't allow him to carry more than one textbook at a time.

'Can you believe she's on the market? I never thought I'd get a shot,' Gregory Marull, star forward on the basketball team, said from two lockers down.

'What's the deal? She has to have cut him loose, am I right?' a guy whose voice Jason didn't recognize asked. 'Moreau's not stupid enough to have bounced her.'

Jason could hardly believe what he was hearing. They were talking about Sienna. Well, about Sienna and Brad who, from the sound of things, had broken up!

Well, that explained a few things – Brad's die-Jason-die look, for one. Brad obviously blamed Jason, at least to some degree, for whatever had gone down between him and Sienna. And Zach, Maggie and Van Dyke were right there with Brad, going by the freeze-out Jason had just received.

He wondered whether Sienna had actually mentioned him as her reason for wanting to split from Brad. Jason slammed his locker closed. He hated to think that Brad blamed him. He'd never wanted to hurt Brad. The guy was his friend.

Slow down, he warned himself. If Sienna had

decided to break it off with Brad because of Jason, nobody had told him about it. Sienna hadn't hurled herself into his arms when he pulled into the parking lot or anything. *Unfortunately!* Jason couldn't help adding in the privacy of his own head.

He knew he needed to talk to her and hoped he'd get the chance at lunch. On the other hand, he realized he'd look like such a vulture sliding up next to her table under the circumstances. And he didn't want to give Brad any more reason to hate him.

Jason let out a frustrated sigh. He'd just have to wait until English. He sat right behind Sienna in that class. They always talked a little before it started. It would only seem normal if they did today.

Yes, it was definitely better to wait. It's not like it would kill him. After all, a crossbow bolt hadn't.

Sienna was already in her seat when Jason walked into English. *OK, here goes*, Jason thought.

'Hey, how are you feeling?' she asked quickly, before he could even sit down. She put on a smile that looked bright, but also brittle – as if it would shatter into lipstick-coated bits of glass at any second.

'You seem a lot better than you did on Monday. I wanted to stop by and see you yesterday, but then we heard about Dominic, and Belle really needed me,' Sienna went on.

'Yeah, of course,' Jason answered. 'How's she doing?'

'She had to leave school this morning,' Sienna answered. 'I guess you saw her break down in assembly.'

Jason nodded.

'I'm trying to think of something to do for her – something everybody can do,' Sienna told him, pushing her long, silky hair back from her face. 'Not a sympathy card, something else. Something . . .' She shook her head. 'Something that doesn't exist, basically.'

'I don't think anything will really take her mind off Dominic right now,' Jason agreed.

'Maybe I'll just try to get her really involved in prepping for the masked ball,' Sienna murmured thoughtfully. 'My mom's determined that it's going to happen, and that means it probably will.' Sienna rolled her eyes, looking for a moment like her usual teasing self. 'Maybe it would be good for Belle and me to bury ourselves in the million and one chores I know Mom will be happy to give us.'

'Anything's good if it keeps her from moping around the house,' Jason said. 'I know when my grandfather died I needed a distraction. Whenever I was alone, I just kept dwelling on things.'

'Exactly,' Sienna agreed. 'I want to try and take Belle out of herself, you know?'

They were interrupted by Ms Hoffman tapping Jason on the shoulder. 'The detectives want to talk to you next,' she told him. 'They're using the principal's office.'

He stood up. 'Should I take my book or . . . ?'

'You might as well,' Ms Hoffman said. 'Just in case.'

'Bye,' Sienna mouthed as Jason turned for the door.

He tried to get his brain away from Sienna and on to Dominic during his short walk to the principal's office.

'Hey, it's Lucky,' Tamburo greeted Jason when he walked through the door. Carson must be on a break, Jason decided. The younger detective was alone in the room.

'I don't feel exactly lucky anymore,' Jason said.

'You're alive, another kid's dead. You're lucky in my book.' Tamburo gestured for Jason to take a seat on the couch in front of the principal's desk, while he half-sat, half-leaned on the desktop. 'So take me through your story one more time.'

'I already told you everything I can remember,' Jason said. 'I haven't thought of anything new.'

'Sometimes just talking brings up things you

thought you'd forgotten,' Tamburo said. 'Besides, you were pretty out of it in the hospital.'

'OK. Whatever I can do to help,' Jason said. He made sure to describe every second of what had happened on the beach: what he saw on the jog, getting back to his beach junk, the sun in his eyes. Then bending down, feeling the impact of the crossbow bolt, stumbling backwards and blacking out.

'You were facing which way when the bolt hit you?' Tamburo asked when Jason had finished the story.

'I don't know. West, I guess,' Jason replied.

The detective looked at him for a long moment, his expression thoughtful. 'You really don't remember anything new, do you?'

Jason shrugged. 'Sorry I can't be more helpful,' he said. 'Were there any similarities between my case and Dominic's?'

'Hard to say, Lucky,' Tamburo replied. 'Since Dominic isn't here to tell us what happened. There weren't any witnesses that we know of. That's why I'm focusing on you. You're our best chance to catch this killer.'

Jason didn't answer. If he was their best chance, that didn't seem very promising. He hadn't seen a thing.

'Don't sweat it,' Tamburo said. 'You're from Michigan, right?'

'Michigan, yeah,' Jason agreed.

'I've never been there,' Tamburo said. 'I heard about these kids in Kansas, though. They moved on from paintball – you ever play paintball?'

'I played once last summer,' Jason answered, confused.

'Anyway, these yahoos, they got bored with it. Seemed a little too tame to them. So they moved on to guns – with blanks, of course.' Tamburo shoved himself away from the desk and dropped down on the couch next to Jason. 'One of them ended up killing his buddy. You can kill someone with a blank if you're close enough. Not everyone knows that.'

Jason raised his eyebrows. 'Yeah, I never knew that,' he admitted.

'I need to ask you something, and you're not going to like it,' Tamburo said. 'But do you think something like that could be happening around here – with crossbows?'

'I don't think one of my friends shot me with a crossbow in some kind of game. Or that Dominic got killed like that, no,' Jason replied.

'You sure?' Tamburo pressed. 'I've seen things like this before, where some kind of fraternity prank goes wrong.'

'That's not what this is,' Jason said, shaking his head.

Tamburo grinned and nodded. 'You know what, Lucky? I don't think so either.' He put his motorcycle boots up on the coffee table. 'So tell me, how well did you know Dominic?'

Jason was surprised at the sudden change of subject. Apparently Detective Tamburo liked to mix things up a bit. 'Not very well,' he replied. 'I'm better friends with his girlfriend, Belle.'

'Oh, really?' Tamburo raised his eyebrows.

'Yeah. Well, Dominic is . . . was . . . kinda hard to get along with,' Jason said slowly. 'He had a temper.'

'And what about you? You got a temper?' Tamburo asked.

'Not like that,' Jason answered honestly.

'So you didn't like him?' Tamburo pressed.

'I didn't say that,' Jason replied. 'Does it matter?'

'Maybe,' Tamburo said mildly. 'I'm just trying to figure you out. I'd like to know if there's anything about you and Dominic that's similar.'

'Oh.' Jason thought about it for a moment. 'Actually, I'd say that Dominic and I were about as different as two people can be,' he said finally.

Tamburo nodded. 'Well, that's going to make my job harder.'

'How?' Jason asked.

'I'm looking for a motive,' Tamburo explained. 'Most killers follow some kind of pattern. So far, the only pattern I'm finding is his weapon of choice. Otherwise the two attacks are completely different. And so are the two victims.'

'Well, we're both guys,' Jason said.

A slow smile spread across Tamburo's face. 'You got a point there, Lucky. That does narrow things down by about fifty per cent. The killer doesn't like girls.'

'Or else he *only* likes girls,' Jason replied.

'Good point,' Tamburo chuckled. 'Well, you can go on back to class. You know where to find me if anything else comes into your head.'

'You don't think he'll strike again, do you?' Jason asked, standing up slowly. The wound in his chest had begun to throb.

'I don't know, Lucky,' Tamburo said. 'Probably. So do me a favor, will you? Remember what I told you about those kids in Kansas.'

Jason stared at him blankly. 'Why?'

'Because you can never be sure where an attack might come from,' Tamburo said. 'It could come from your friends. You keep an eye on them and remember that you never know what's going on beneath the surface.'

'I know none of my friends is a killer,' Jason said firmly.

'I hope you're right,' the detective replied.

Jason turned to go, wishing he'd had something – anything – to say that would help catch the crossbow killer.

'And Jason,' Tamburo said quietly from behind him. 'Don't worry. I'll get him.'

EIGHT

Jason headed directly to the pool, skipping the locker room all together, since he didn't have to change out of his street clothes. And, OK, because he didn't want to deal with all the gossip that would be flying around in there. Especially since today there would be two big topics: one, Brad and Sienna; and two, the crossbow killer. Jason didn't want to hear or think about either of them right now.

He stared into the ultra-blue water of DeVere's Olympic-standard pool. He wanted to dive in. He didn't know how he was going to survive two months without swimming. He knew he'd miss the adrenalin rush of the relay, and the total *otherness* of even just swimming laps. Swimming was a time-out for him. In the water, Jason became almost another creature – all body, or maybe all soul. There was no thought, no worries. Just movement. Water. And silence.

Priesmeyer and a couple of the other divers were

first out of the locker room. 'Jason, good to see you breathing, dude,' Priesmeyer said as he sat down with his crew.

'Good to *be* breathing,' Jason answered.

Priesmeyer was one of the most devoted guys on the team. He not only shaved his legs and his pits for ultimate slide through the water, he shaved his head. He probably didn't care all that much about the Brad and Sienna break-up. He probably cared even less whether or not Jason had any part in the split. It wasn't as if he was one of the vampires, who mostly seemed to have closed ranks against Jason.

'I hope this meeting's short,' Priesmeyer said. 'My two-and-a-half-pike dive was for crap last time. I need to put in some serious time on it today.'

'I don't know why we have to be here anyway,' Wes Duffy, another of the divers, complained. 'It's all going to be about how the coach handles the medley without you, Freeman. There's no one else who can take on your position. Everyone else is at least six seconds behind your breaststroke time.'

'Not everybody,' Brad commented as he and Van Dyke joined the group. He wore his typical friendly smile, but he didn't even glance in Jason's direction, and his voice had an undercurrent of coldness to it.

Not enough for anyone else to notice, Jason thought, *just enough to make it clear to me that I'm on his shit list.*

'Not nearly everybody,' Van Dyke agreed, cheerfully.

'Meaning you two, right?' Wes said. 'Either of you could cover Jason's slot in the medley, sure. But if either of you *did*, that would still leave one leg of the relay empty. So, I'm basically right. There's no one to take his spot.'

'It might take a little time,' Brad answered. 'But we have to look at the big picture. We need a long-term solution. There were a few good swimmers that didn't make the cut. I'm sure we can get one of them up to speed.'

Brad didn't even bother to acknowledge Jason as he said this. It was like Jason was off the team permanently – and not even in the room.

'Yeah, Brad pretty much held Freeman's hand from day one,' Van Dyke put in. 'Anyone who gets that kind of treatment isn't going to have a problem on the medley team. Brad and I do the heavy lifting.'

'Uh, Jason and I. Right here!' Harberts reminded him. Harberts was the other member of the four-person relay team.

'No offence, Harberts,' Van Dyke said. 'You know we wouldn't be number one without you. Those competitions can get pretty intense. We need someone to make us laugh – you know, break the tension.'

Everybody laughed, knowing it was just trash talk. The guys on the team liked to insult one another for fun, but they all knew just how good each and every person on the team was when it came time to compete.

Harberts shook his head good-naturedly. 'Thanks. Thanks very much. Just let me go get my big rubber nose and my polka-dot fins,' he said, but he grinned as he spoke.

Jason forced a smile too. He wasn't going to let any-one on the team see that Brad and Van Dyke giving him the freeze-out bothered him. Even though it did.

Jason remembered that Brad *had* practically held his hand the first day of practice. He'd introduced Jason to everyone. And later he'd invited Jason to his first DeVere Heights party. Brad had been one of Jason's first friends at the new school.

And now Jason had clearly lost him as a friend – for good.

Jason took a pull on his Jones' WhoopAss. Like any energy drink was really going to make him feel better about the day he'd had.

'Yeah, so Brad definitely doesn't want me back on

the team – ever,' he told Adam, who sat across the
kitchen table with his own WhoopAss. 'He kept talking
about long-term solutions for the medley team, like
I'm never going to heal up.' Jason set the drink back on
the table, though it was quite hard to find space since
Dani had her astrology charts spread out all over the
place.

'It's not really up to him though, right?' Adam
asked. 'The coach will make the call once you're ready
to swim again.'

'Yeah,' Dani agreed. 'Hey, does this look like a
stellium?' She pointed to a spot on her planetary chart.

'If I knew what a stellium was, I'd tell you,' Adam
answered.

'It's a conjunction of three or more planets. And a
conjunction before you ask is when the planets are at
the same degree or really close. When that happens it
creates a major energy,' Dani explained. 'If this is a
stellium, it changes my whole reading. It means that
the guy I'm looking for is going to be more of a Johnny
Depp than a Brad Pitt. I think.'

'It looks like a conjunction to me,' Adam told her.
Dani scribbled something in her notebook, and Adam
turned back to Jason. 'As for you, I bet your horoscope
couldn't have been all bad for today. Brad and

Sienna broke up. Talk about long-term solutions . . .'

Dani's head came up. Jason shot her a you-speak-you-die look and his sister reluctantly returned her attention to her charts.

'Yeah, but I think right now what Sienna needs most is a friend. Just a friend,' Jason told Adam.

'But long term?' Adam pushed.

'Long term? I don't even know if I should be thinking about long term right now,' Jason said. 'I don't even know why Brad and Sienna—'

'Hey, this is kind of weird,' Dani interrupted. 'You and Dominic were both attacked on the first evening of a new lunar cycle,' she told Jason, shoving a different chart toward the boys.

'Really?' Adam asked, eyebrows lifted in surprise. 'That's interesting.'

'Wait. You two have left me behind. My brain works on the *normal* frequency, remember?' Jason announced.

'In many belief systems the beginning of a new lunar cycle is a time of great ritual significance,' Dani explained, just as her cell began to play some Enya song. She pulled the phone out of her purse and checked the screen. 'Billy,' she told them. 'Adam, you finish educating him.'

As soon as Dani left the room, Adam started talking, low and fast. 'Want to know something else about the lunar cycle?' he muttered. 'When I was researching vampires, I found out that the guys who used to hunt them would begin hunting at the time of a new moon and end when the moon was full. I think we have to seriously consider that the crossbow killer is hunting down vampires.'

'These are the hunters who used to work in Medieval Europe, right?' Jason asked.

'Yeah,' Adam said. 'And if I'm right, they're now working in modern-day Malibu.'

'Adam . . .' Jason shook his head. 'Why do you have such a hard time remembering that I, probably your closest friend, am not a friend of Dracula?'

'You ever hear that expression "if it looks like a duck and it quacks like a duck, it's probably a duck"?' Adam asked.

'Yeah. So?'

'Well, you swim with the vampires, you party with the vampires, you make out with one special vampire – so maybe to the hunter you looked like a duck. I mean, vampire,' Adam said.

'But these vampire hunters of yours, don't they have any Spidey senses? Can't they, like, smell a vampire at a couple of hundred feet or anything?' Jason asked. 'I mean, obviously I *am* astonishingly good-looking. But I'm not quite vampiric in that department, you know?'

'Well, riddle me this,' Adam replied calmly. 'Do you have a better explanation for why somebody shot you with a freakin' crossbow?'

At one o'clock in the morning, Jason was lying in bed, staring up at the ceiling, still trying to come up with an answer to Adam's question: *'Do you have a better explanation for why somebody shot you with a freakin' crossbow?'*

Jason didn't have a better explanation, but some things didn't *have* explanations. Some things were just random. And evil.

Jason closed his eyes. And something black slid across his eyelids, a deeper darkness that appeared for a second, then was gone. Jason snapped his eyes open. The shadow slipped along the ceiling and back again.

The tree branch, Jason told himself. *It's the shadow of the branch waving in the wind. Get a grip.*

He knew it was just his brain playing tricks on him. Almost getting killed did that to you, set your imagination running in all sorts of nasty directions.

But the shadow had reminded him of something real – he just couldn't quite remember what.

Jason closed his eyes again. But just as he was about to slide into sleep, his body gave a jerk, and he was wide awake. And now he remembered. The shadow had reminded him of being back in the alley by the pawn shop. He'd been there to buy back the chalice – the vampire relic that Tyler had stolen – and someone had seen him. A shadowy figure. A man. Jason wondered if that man had been deliberately watching to see who came for the chalice, guessing that if the vampires wanted it back, they'd send a vampire to fetch it. Because, if so, it would be easy enough to see why he'd have assumed Jason was a vampire – and it suddenly made Adam's 'duck' scenario look a lot more credible.

Jason punched Tyler's number into his cell as he pushed his tray down the metal track next to the row of food in the cafeteria. He took a slice of pesto pizza as the phone began to ring and grabbed a bottle of Borba anti-aging water – just because he thought that if Sienna saw him drinking it she'd smile, and Jason thought she could use a smile.

Tyler's voicemail picked up as Jason paid for his food. It announced that the mail box was full.

Frowning, Jason pocketed his cell and headed to his usual table on the terrace. Adam was already there.

'What's up, bro?'

'I just tried to get Tyler on the phone,' Jason said as he sat down. 'No luck. I haven't talked to him since he left for Michigan. I just wanted to make sure he's OK.'

'He's got to be a lot more OK there than he was here,' Adam answered. 'There are no fanged types after him in Michigan.'

'True.' Jason took a bite of his pizza. 'Last night I was thinking about the, you know, the *cup* that Tyler stole. When I went to buy it back from the pawn shop, I thought there was somebody watching me. Then this truck went by and they were gone, and I decided I must have imagined it. But now, I'm thinking maybe it could have been the crossbow killer. And if it was, then maybe—'

'That's why the killer thinks you're a V!' Adam finished for him excitedly. 'Because the killer saw you buying the relic. Do you remember anything about him, anything at all?'

Jason shook his head. 'It's practically all I've been thinking about. I spaced out in every class. At least the teachers are cutting me some slack because I almost died and everything.' He rubbed some grit out of the corner of one eye. 'But I came up with nothing. The guy was in the shadows. I only saw him for a moment. What about your dad and the detectives? Have you heard anything? They getting close at all?'

'No. And my dad's not exactly easy to live with right now,' Adam told him. 'I wish I could tell him about my V-hunter theory, but if I did I'd be talking to you from a padded cell for the next decade or so.'

'If your theory's right, does that mean there will be more killing before the lunar cycle ends?' Jason asked, his eyes immediately seeking out Sienna at her usual table. Her usual table without Brad, today. Or Dominic, ever again.

'From what I've read, the killing goes on between the new moon and the full moon. Then it's closed season until the next month's new moon,' Adam explained. 'It's not good karma, or whatever, to hunt during the waning moon, when the full moon is diminishing. The hunt is supposed to be especially powerful if there is a kill on the day of the new moon – which there was – and on the day of the full moon, which is coming up on the fifteenth.'

'So you're saying we could be looking at a killing spree lasting ten more days?' Jason asked. His spine felt like it had been turned into a lightning rod, a lightning rod during a massive thunderstorm.

'Yeah.' For once, Adam seemed to have run out of words.

What are we going to do? Jason thought. What *could* they do? He had no info to give Tamburo and Carson. He could hardly tell them to go after a shadowy figure who may or may not have been watching him several weeks ago.

'Hey, Freeman,' a voice interrupted Jason's thoughts, and he glanced up to see Van Dyke looming over their table.

'Hey,' Jason said, surprised the guy was even talking to him. Van Dyke had been ignoring Jason all week. He seemed to think it was his duty as Brad's best friend.

'Listen, man, I was thinking about your wound,' Van Dyke said. 'You know, and how you can't swim.'

'Only until February,' Jason replied.

'Yeah, well, if you can't swim you probably can't dance, either,' Van Dyke said.

'That must be my excuse!' Adam put in, cheerfully talking around a curly fry in his mouth. 'If only I'd taken more swimming lessons, I'd be like John Travolta on the dance floor.'

Van Dyke ignored him, keeping his eyes on Jason. 'Dancing might open up your stitches, right?'

'I guess it's possible . . .' Jason replied cautiously. He had no idea where Van Dyke was going with this, but he had a feeling he wasn't going to like it.

'Right. So you should probably take a pass on the masked ball.' He clapped Jason on the shoulder, and Jason winced in pain. 'Just to be on the safe side.'

Van Dyke ambled away, looking pleased with himself. Jason just shook his head.

'That unfeeling bastard,' Adam said. 'I think he's threatened by you. You're the first human around here to attract a V girl. Think about it. Our friends only date their own. They might suck on us regular folk, but that's it. In terms of couples, there's Brad and Sienna – well, there was. And Belle and . . .' Adam thought better of mentioning that couple and just went on. 'Zach went to the prom with Sienna's sister. Maggie used to go out with Van Dyke. Erin Henry is with Max Vioget. And so it goes. And so it has always gone. Van Dyke and company don't like you shaking up their old world order.'

'I know there are rumors going around that Brad and Sienna split because of me. But Sienna and I aren't together. We've hardly even talked since the break-up,'

Jason told Adam. 'I don't know what's going on with us exactly. But it's not romantic. I don't think she's ready for that. I guess we're what we've always been: friends.'

Adam grinned. 'Maybe for now. But for how long, *amigo*?'

NINE

'To go to swim practice or not go swim practice, that is the question,' Adam said, stopping at Jason's locker after school.

Jason had to smile. He'd been standing there staring at his gym bag for about two minutes, trying to decide whether to head to the pool or not. Obviously Adam had noticed his dilemma. 'I want to support the team,' Jason said. 'But I'm not sure the team is interested in my support.'

'Brad and Van Dyke are not the whole team,' Adam pointed out. 'If you want to go, go.'

Jason sighed. Another afternoon of sitting on the bleachers and getting ignored by his so-called friends? It was sure to be a major downer. 'You know what?' he said. 'I've had enough depression for one day. I think I'll blow off practice. You want to hit Eddie's?'

'Can't do it, my man,' Adam replied. 'My mom is making me help write the Christmas cards this year.

She's got this whole thing set up for today – stacks of cards, tons of stamps, a huge list of names. It's like hell. Only with lots of holiday cheer.'

Jason grimaced. 'Sorry.'

'Yeah. She promised I could eat Christmas cookies the whole time, though, so it's not a total loss.' Adam yanked his backpack up higher on his shoulder and headed off with a wave.

Jason swung the locker door shut and turned toward the exit. Now that he'd decided not to go to practice, he wasn't sure what to do. Going home wasn't an appetizing option; his mother would be certain he'd skipped practice because his wound was giving him trouble, and she'd send him straight to bed and make sure he stayed there. And going to Eddie's by himself didn't seem like much fun, either.

'Christmas shopping,' he muttered. 'After all, it's got to be done sometime.' The idea of wandering around the mall hunting for suitable gifts was kind of daunting, but it beat anything else Jason could think of.

By the time he reached the mall, he was in a better mood. It was nice to get away from school and all the negativity there. The mall wasn't too crowded, and the hallways were all decorated in pinecone-strewn garlands and twinkling white lights, with humongous bushy poinsettias everywhere. Tasteful carols played softly through the P.A. system – no *Frosty the Snowman* here in Malibu. It was all *Hallelujah Chorus* type stuff. Jason couldn't help himself – he was getting into the spirit. Only a Grinch would be able to resist this idyllic yuletide setting. Smiling, he headed for Tower Records.

'I don't believe it. The Michigan boy actually shops!'

Jason stopped in his tracks. *Sienna*. He steeled himself to meet her eyes and turned around.

She looked stunning. Tight, dark blue jeans and an adorable pink ski sleeveless jacket – as if it was really cold enough out to need a jacket. Still, she made it look perfectly sensible, like she might have to fly off to Aspen on a moment's notice.

Just friends, Jason told himself. *We're just friends.* 'Of course I shop,' he said.

Sienna smiled. 'Guys usually hate the mall. It's generally a female-only zone until about two p.m. on Christmas Eve. Then the men all swoop in to do their typical last-minute gift shopping.'

'Well . . .' Jason felt his cheeks heat up.

'I knew it!' Sienna cried, delighted. 'That's your usual M.O. isn't it?'

'You got me. I hate shopping. I especially hate shopping for presents. How am I supposed to know what my mother wants? Or my sister?' Jason shook his head. 'They're so picky about what they wear, what they eat, how they smell. I'm afraid to buy them anything. I'm sure to get it wrong somehow.'

'So what are you doing here? Torturing yourself?' Sienna teased.

'If I'd wanted torture I'd have gone to swim practice,' Jason joked. Sienna's smile vanished instantly and he sighed. Why had he brought up the swim team? Obviously it would make Sienna think of Brad. How could he be so stupid?

Sienna gazed down at her feet for a moment, and there was an awkward silence.

'I figured I'd hit the music store first and grab a couple of CDs for my dad,' Jason said. 'He's the easy one to buy for in my family. He has this thing for old doo-wop songs from the fifties. It's totally weird, but it makes things simple. There must've been hundreds of doo-wop bands, because I can always find a CD he doesn't have.' Jason felt a little stupid. He was babbling, trying to cover up the awkwardness between them, but all he'd managed to do was make things more awkward. It was obviously time for a different tactic.

'Anyway, where's Belle?' he asked, looking around. 'I thought she was your constant shopping companion.'

'Um, she's down in Mexico, in Cabo,' Sienna said quietly. 'Her mom wanted to get her out of here for a while. She's pretty freaked out about Dominic.'

Jason winced. He'd been trying to change the subject to lighten the mood, but instead he'd just made it even worse. 'Of course she is.' He shook his head. 'I'm sorry. I didn't mean to . . .' He let his words tail off, unsure what to say.

Sienna shrugged. 'Don't worry about it. Nobody's thinking straight these days.'

'It's good that Belle has the chance to get away. Maybe it'll help,' Jason suggested.

'Yeah, she and Dominic have been together since seventh grade,' Sienna answered. 'She doesn't know what to do with herself now that he's gone.'

'That's terrible,' Jason said. Dominic had always seemed like kind of a jerk to him, but that didn't mean the guy deserved to die. And no matter how he'd acted, Belle had obviously loved him. 'Poor Belle. I can't even imagine how it must feel to lose someone you've been with for so long.'

Sienna didn't answer. Jason wondered if she was thinking about Brad. They'd been together for years, too.

'So when is Belle coming back?' he asked. 'Is she going to miss Dominic's funeral?'

'No, she'll be back for that,' Sienna replied. 'I know Belle will want to come home for the funeral.' She ran her hand through her long, dark hair. 'You know what? I'm sick of this,' she announced.

'Sick of what?' Jason asked.

'Feeling this way.' Sienna dropped down onto one of the wrought-iron benches that lined the hallway. 'I'm sick of being sad and scared, and I'm sick of crying and worrying. I just want everything to go back to normal.'

Jason sat down next to her. 'I know what you mean.'

'Sorry. I don't mean to whine. And I know it hasn't even been for long. But I just feel like my whole life has suddenly changed and it's never going to change back,' Sienna said. 'How are you doing? Everything healing up OK?'

'So far, so good,' Jason assured her. 'My chest aches sometimes, but I can handle it.'

Sienna leaned back and gazed at the tall pine tree at the end of the hall. It was decorated with red bows and white lights, and a pile of fake presents was artfully arranged around its base. 'Christmastime is my favorite part of the year,' she said. 'I hate that it's been ruined.'

'I know what you mean. Usually right around now is when the holiday spirit really kicks in for me,' Jason said. 'Of course, usually right around now is when the weather starts getting super cold and there's snow. In Michigan.'

'We don't do the whole white Christmas thing here,' Sienna said. 'The closest you're going to get is some fake snow on a movie set.'

'It's hard to get used to,' he said. 'It's not even cold enough to drink hot chocolate. What kind of Christmas spirit can you have without hot chocolate?'

'We are truly pathetic,' Sienna agreed. 'Tell you what. Let's make it our mission to get ourselves into the Christmas spirit. Today. Here. Now.'

'I *was* starting to feel it for a second with the carols and everything,' Jason admitted. 'Maybe, if we both wish very, very hard . . .' He clasped his hands together and did his best imitation of a kid from a holiday special.

'Yes! Yes, miracles can happen!' Sienna answered, in a high childlike voice. 'For starters, I can help you with your Christmas shopping,' she offered in her usual tone. 'I don't claim to even know what doo-wop is, but I can definitely pick out stuff for your mom and Dani.'

'Really? You'd do that?' Jason felt his mood lifting already.

'Sure. But we have to make a pact. Nothing depressing,' Sienna said. 'As long as we're in the mall, we're in a no-reality zone. I don't want to think about Dominic, or Belle, or . . . anything else.'

Brad, Jason thought. *That's what she means. She doesn't want to think about their break-up. Well, that's just fine with me.* 'It's a deal,' he said. 'We're all about the unreality.'

'Good. Then let's go,' Sienna said, standing up.

'Where do we start?' Jason asked.

'Bloomingdales for your mom. Then Armani Exchange for Dani,' Sienna said. 'Or maybe Fendi. I haven't decided yet.'

'You're already speaking a foreign language as far as I'm concerned,' Jason joked. He stood up too.

'Just pay close attention to me and I'll have you shopping like a pro in no time,' she promised.

Pay close attention to Sienna? That shouldn't be a problem, Jason thought as he followed her toward Bloomies. Shopping with Sienna wasn't actually as easy as Jason had thought it might be. In Bloomingdales, Sienna decided that perfume was the way to go for his mother. So she made Jason do a bunch of smell tests of different scents – which meant he had to try and stand still while Sienna waved the inside of her slender wrist under his nose, or lifted her hair and offered her delicate neck for him to sniff. All of which tested to the limit Jason's resolve to be nothing more than friends with Sienna for the time being.

'You like this one?' she asked, spritzing on yet another scent.

He sniffed at her and made a face, pretending to hold his nose.

Sienna laughed and swatted his arm. 'Fine. I'll just pick one.'

'How can you tell?' he asked. 'Your left arm smells of one thing, your right arm smells of another. You're like one of my sister's fashion magazines – every page has some different perfumed card on it, so the whole thing just smells weird.'

'I don't know whether I should be more worried that you clearly spend a lot of your time reading fashion magazines, or that you think I smell weird!' Sienna teased.

Jason tried to protest and explain that that wasn't what he'd meant, but she just laughed at him and held out a tiny bottle of perfume.

'This one,' she told him.

He took it over to the cashier without bothering to smell it. If Sienna said it was the right one, that was good enough for him.

'Let's do one of your gifts next,' he suggested. 'Who do you need to buy for?'

'Well, the hardest one is my dad,' she told him. 'Every year I manage to pick him something he doesn't need or want.'

'What are his hobbies?' Jason asked.

'Complaining about how much money my sister and I spend,' Sienna replied. 'That's about it.'

'I've got it!' Jason replied. 'The perfect gift: a money clip.'

'Michigan!' Sienna cried. 'I'm impressed. That's a great idea. There's a Tiffany's in this mall. They've got to have silver money clips.'

'You could even get it engraved,' Jason suggested.

'Look at you,' she cooed. 'Thinking like a shopper already. I'm so proud!'

'Yeah, well, just don't tell anyone,' Jason said. 'I have a reputation to protect.'

'Oh, really? What reputation is that?'

'The one where I'm clueless about stores and shopping – like all the other guys,' Jason replied.

'Your secret is safe with me,' Sienna promised, leading the way to Tiffany's.

Jason wandered around the store while Sienna talked to the clerk about engraving. He couldn't help noticing that there didn't seem to be a single thing in the whole place for less than a hundred bucks.

'Shopping for your girlfriend?' one of the salesladies asked him. 'She's lovely.'

'Oh, no, she's not my girlfriend,' Jason said quickly, shooting a glance at Sienna. 'Yet,' he added.

The saleslady laughed. 'That's the spirit! Well, if you want to win her over, you might think about getting her some jewelry. We have a lovely friendship ring . . .'

'Friendship?' Jason glanced into the case at the ring she was pointing to. The ring was a delicate band of gold and silver intertwined. It would look perfect on Sienna's hand. 'I guess I could get her a *friendship* ring for Christmas,' he mused.

'Ready?' Sienna asked, coming up behind him.

Jason jumped, and exchanged a meaningful look with the saleslady. 'Sure,' he said. 'Maybe I'll come back another day,' he murmured as Sienna headed for the door.

'I'll keep the ring for you,' the saleslady replied quietly with a smile.

'Let's go to Black Cherry for your sister,' Sienna said as they left Tiffany's. 'It's this great little boutique that has a bunch of different designers.'

Half an hour and one beaded evening purse later – and Sienna was clearly just getting into her stride. 'How about your Aunt Bianca next?' she suggested, looking around for a suitable store. 'Did you have anything special in mind for her?'

'I think I need a break from shopping,' Jason admitted. 'I feel a little overwhelmed.'

She gave him one of her long, sideways looks. 'I forgot I'm dealing with a virgin,' she teased. 'You're obviously not ready for a full afternoon of shopping.'

'Sorry,' Jason said with a grin. 'Hey, how about we just refuel?' he suggested. 'Food court?' He'd been having such a good time with Sienna that he'd actually managed to forget about his wound for awhile. And he hadn't thought about Dominic or the situation at school, either. He was in no hurry to call an end to the whole Christmas shopping experience – just the shopping part.

'Sounds good,' Sienna agreed, and led the way, swinging her small purse as she walked. Jason felt happy just watching her. She seemed in a much better mood than she had before. Clearly their mission to get into the Christmas spirit was working. 'What do you want to eat? Sushi? Or they have a pretty decent salad place here.'

'No. No way,' Jason replied firmly. 'I've had it with classy things. It's holiday time, and this is a mall.

There's supposed to be a guy dressed in a badly fitting Santa suit, and multicolored Christmas lights all over the place, all clashing with each other. And there should be really loud, really cheesy music playing. None of this lovely classical stuff – it should be *Rudolph* and *Frosty* and *Grandma Got Run Over By a Reindeer.*'

Sienna wrinkled her perfect nose, but her dark eyes danced with amusement. 'Is that what the holidays are like in the flyover states?' she asked.

'That's what the holidays are like all over America. Don't kid yourself,' he said. 'You Malibu kids live in a little bubble.'

'Probably true,' Sienna admitted with a laugh. 'So where does that leave us, food-wise?'

'Well, what we need is something really down home to counterbalance all this snootiness,' Jason said. He studied all the options in the upscale food court. It wouldn't be easy to find typical mall junk food in this place. 'There!' he cried. 'Hot Dog on a Stick!'

Sienna's mouth dropped open. 'You are kidding, right?'

'Nope. We're having corn dogs,' Jason said. 'Come on.'

'I thought that place was banned for anyone over the age of eight,' Sienna told him.

'You've never had a corn dog, have you?' Jason asked.

She shook her head.

'Oh, you are in for a treat.' He walked up to the counter and grinned at the guy in the paper hat. 'Two corn dogs. Oh, and an American cheese thing. My treat,' he added to Sienna.

'It better be,' she joked. 'I don't think I'm up to paying for food that comes on a stick.'

Jason handed her one of the dogs. 'You're going to eat those words. Corn dogs are the best things ever.'

Sienna stared at it in dismay. 'How am I supposed to eat it?'

'However you want. That's half the fun.' Jason took a humongous bite right off the top of his, letting the sweet fried cornbread melt in his mouth before chewing up the hot dog inside.

Sienna went another way. She took a tiny taste of the cornbread. 'Yum,' she purred. 'I see what you mean.' She began to carefully nibble all the way around the hot dog, taking itty-bitty bites. 'That *is* good.'

Jason winked at her playfully, as if to say 'I told you so!'

'What's that cheese thing?' she asked when she finished her hot dog. 'Give me some.'

'I thought you disapproved of food on sticks,' he teased her as she devoured American cheese on a stick.

'That also comes in spicy jack cheese with a saucy jalapeño flavor that I think your palate will love.'

'You've converted me. I want everything on a stick from now on.' Sienna said, licking her lips. 'What else is there? Popsicles . . .'

'Shish kebabs,' he added.

'All kinds of satay at the Indian place,' Sienna said.

'Then there's the fruit category,' Jason put in. 'Chocolate-covered bananas on sticks. Caramel apples.'

Sienna was laughing. 'You've opened my eyes to a whole new world of culinary delights.'

'See? Being cheesy has its charms,' Jason told her.

'If only there was some *Rudolph* playing, it would be the perfect cheesy Christmas,' Sienna joked. Then her expression grew serious. 'Thank you.'

'For what?' Jason asked.

'For this – our afternoon away from all the depressing things that have been going on,' Sienna sighed. 'It's been a hard week. I haven't had anyone to talk to about . . . anything.'

Once again, Jason had the feeling that she was talking about Brad. Between their break-up and Belle's going off to Mexico, Sienna was probably more lonely than usual. He found himself reaching for her hand, and forced himself to stop. *It's too soon*, he thought.

Touching Sienna at the moment seemed wrong. She might think he was making a move on her since she was suddenly single. And he didn't want to be that guy – the guy that Brad and Van Dyke and all the other vampires apparently thought he was. He hoped that if he just waited until it was clear that Sienna hadn't broken up with Brad because of him, they'd all be able to be friends again. And then, when things had calmed down, maybe he and Sienna could think about dating. But for now, everything had to stay as it was.

Sienna was watching him closely. She had to have seen his hesitation about touching her, but she didn't say anything. Instead she just smiled at him. 'Think you're rested enough to hit Armani Exchange for your aunt now? I won't be able to rest until I've got you through your entire Christmas shopping list.'

'Let's do it,' Jason said with a grin.

As they wandered back out into the hallway, Jason felt as if he'd lost about fifty pounds. Things were still strained with Brad, but at least he and Sienna were getting along well. She still took his breath away, but it didn't matter. They were friends. Just friends. Sooner or later, Brad would realize that and things would get back to normal. Wouldn't they?

TEN

'Do you think this skirt is too short for a funeral?' Dani asked on Saturday morning. Her black, flowing skirt skimmed her knees.

'It looks OK to me,' Jason replied, straightening the jacket of his one and only suit. 'And if we don't leave now, we'll be late.'

Dani frowned at her reflection in the hall mirror. 'I guess I don't have time to change.'

'Why do you want to come, anyway?' Jason said. 'It will only make you sad, and you hardly even knew Dominic. You don't have to do this.'

'Like you were such great friends with him.' Dani rolled her eyes. 'You're only going because you want to see Sienna.'

'I'm going because it's the right thing to do,' Jason replied seriously. 'And I doubt anyone's even going to notice what you're wearing.'

'Untrue. It'll be like a fashion show,' Dani told him,

pulling open the front door and heading out to the VW. 'There aren't any parties this weekend, so everyone's going to treat this funeral as an excuse to look good.'

'That's not funny,' Jason replied.

Dani turned to him, her eyes sad. 'I know,' she said. 'I don't mean that people don't care about Dominic's death. But face it, we live in an image-conscious world. And this is Malibu! People will be mourning and primping at the same time.'

Jason hoped she was wrong, but it turned out his little sister understood things better than he did this time. Dominic's funeral – which was taking place at an oh-so-sophisticated and elegant funeral mansion – was packed with what appeared to be the entire population of Malibu, and they were all dressed to the nines. The men wore dark suits, but they were well-cut and expensive-looking suits. And most of the women were in beautiful little black dresses. Even Jason could see that they'd all spent a lot of time on their hair and make-up. It was the best-dressed funeral he'd ever attended.

The vampires looked the most splendid of all, of course. They were all decked out in Italian suits and couture dresses, and they kept to themselves, sitting in a group at the front of the funeral hall. A few of the older women were wearing wide-brimmed black hats, and Dominic's mother wore a black silk veil over her face. Belle sat nearby, dark glasses covering her eyes. She twisted her hands together in her lap, her usually smiling mouth turned down, her chin trembling.

Jason spotted Sienna sitting with her parents next to Zach Lafrenière and his family. Brad was in the next row back.

Aaron Harberts walked by with Priesmeyer. He slapped Jason on the back as he passed. 'Hey, Freeman!'

'Hey.'

'I hear everyone's heading out to the beach after the service. You coming?' Harberts asked.

'Definitely,' Dani answered for Jason.

'What's up, party people in the place to be?' Adam said, coming up behind them. Dani smirked.

'It's *not* a party,' Jason insisted.

'I know. You're right.' Adam pulled at his tie, looking uncomfortable. 'I'm sorry. I always act inappropriately when I'm nervous.'

Jason nodded. 'It just seems all wrong that Dominic's dead. You're not supposed to die young. You're supposed to get your whole life to live.'

Dani squeezed his arm. 'I see Kristy and Billy. Do you mind if I sit with them?'

'Of course not,' Jason said. She gave him a little smile and took off to join her friends.

'You think I can change before we hit the beach later?' Adam asked.

'Why? Having trouble with your formal wear?' Jason asked, taking in Adam's suit.

'My dad made me wear it,' Adam grumbled. He shot a look at his father, standing in the back of the room with a few uniform cops. Jason was surprised to see Tamburo behind them, leaning against the doorframe. He was the only one in the entire room not dressed in mourning clothes. Instead, he just wore his typical jeans and boots, and he hadn't even bothered to shave.

He's not even pretending that he's here to mourn Dominic, Jason realized. *He's just here to see if anybody acts suspiciously.*

Tamburo's eyes turned to Jason, as if he could feel that Jason was watching him. He gave a casual nod and Jason nodded back. Then Tamburo returned his gaze to the other funeral-goers, studying each one in turn.

'Wow. This really is a big event, huh?' Jason said to Adam. 'Vampires, cops and everything in between.'

'Anyone who's anyone is here,' Adam agreed. 'Personally I'm wondering about the rituals of a vampire funeral. What do you think they do?'

'I think they mourn,' Jason said sharply. 'But then again, most of these people look as if they're just here to be seen, so maybe I'm wrong about that.'

'That's the way it is in Malibu,' Adam said simply. 'Everybody wants to show off, no matter what. It doesn't mean they don't care about Dominic.'

A tall man in a black suit stepped up to the podium and cleared his throat to signal that the service was about to start.

'We better find seats. I don't think us non-dentally enhanced types are welcome over there,' Adam said, nodding at the all-vampire section.

Jason glanced over. It was eerie to see almost all the DeVere Heights families in a block like that. It was kind of like looking at a living sculpture garden. All of them were almost supernaturally beautiful, each in their own individual way. 'Sienna told me that vampires can manipulate their appearance,' he whispered to Adam. 'That their natural appearance is more beautiful than what they show us.'

Adam studied the vampire section. 'Looks like they're letting their true selves shine through for today.'

Jason nodded as he gazed around the place. All the other Malibu people who had come to the funeral, trying so hard to make an impression in their expensive clothes, simply didn't stand a chance. The vampires were stunning, and they didn't seem to have noticed that anybody else was even there.

As the service went on, Jason found himself staring at Sienna. He'd seen her look this gorgeous once before, when she had first told him that she was a vampire. She'd let him see her true beauty then and it was just as mesmerizing now. Her black hair glimmered in the dim light, her skin was sheer golden perfection and, all of a sudden, Jason felt like the biggest idiot in the world.

Why had he ever let himself think that Sienna would want to be with him? Look at her, surrounded by the other-worldly people she belonged to. She was one of them. He wasn't. End of story.

Then she turned. Her dark eyes met his across the sea of faces, and she smiled.

A sizzle raced through Jason's body and all his doubt disappeared. It didn't matter what *she* was or what *he* wasn't. They were made for each other.

'I cannot wait for the weekend,' Dani said from the passenger seat of Jason's Bug on their way to school on Monday. She raked her fingers through her hair, trying to keep the windy convertible from ruining her careful styling.

'It's only Monday,' Jason pointed out. 'Isn't it a little early to be wanting a weekend?'

'Duh. The charity ball is this weekend,' Dani replied. 'And I *know* you have to be interested in that.'

Jason didn't answer. Sienna's family organized the ball every year. It was basically her party. Of course he was interested.

'I finished my star chart yesterday while you were busy working out,' Dani went on. 'Which you totally shouldn't be doing, by the way.'

'I called and checked in with the doctor. She said light exercise would be OK,' Jason protested. 'And I only used five-pound weights.'

'Anyway, the ball is on a great day for me, astrologically speaking,' Dani said. 'It's a perfect romance day!'

'You know all that stuff has no scientific basis,' Jason said. 'I don't think you should count on it. You might be disappointed.'

Dani ignored him. 'Mom said I can go dress shopping with Kristy after school, so I don't need a ride home today,' she told him. 'In fact, I'm supposed to meet Kristy before first period to figure out what stores to hit, so can you step on it?'

Instead, Jason took his foot off the gas. There was a string of brake lights up ahead, all of them snaking in a line toward the gates of DeVere High. He slowed to a stop behind the car in front of them.

'How long do you think they're going to keep up this new security thing?' Dani asked, squinting into the sunlight to try to get a better look.

'Probably until they find the guy who attacked Dominic,' Jason said.

'And you,' Dani said. 'You got attacked, too, remember?'

'How could I forget? Anyway, that's two students attacked. Makes sense they'd want to be careful.'

'Neither one of you was attacked at school, though,' Dani said doubtfully. 'It seems a little extreme.'

The buzzing of a small motor cut through the air and Adam appeared on his Vespa, driving back along the line of cars. When he saw Jason, he stopped.

'You're going the wrong way,' Jason told him.

'I know. The Vespa finally comes in handy!' Adam grinned. 'I don't have to sit in traffic waiting to make a U-turn. I can just scooch through the cars and take this baby on the shoulder.'

'It's still illegal,' Dani grumbled.

'We're all waiting to turn around?' Jason asked. 'I assumed it was the usual I.D. check line.'

Adam's face grew serious. 'I guess you haven't been listening to your radio then,' he said. 'School's closed.'

'What? Why?' Jason cried.

'There's been another murder. Scott Challon.'

'Oh my God!' Dani gasped, her face paling.

Jason had a sinking feeling that he knew what was coming next. 'How did it happen?' he asked.

'Crossbow bolt to the heart,' Adam confirmed, shaking his head. 'They found his body first thing this morning. And since all the victims so far are DeVere High students, Detective Tamburo wanted to sweep the school for anything that might lead to a suspect.'

'I see Maria's car up ahead,' Dani said. 'She drives Kristy in to school in the mornings. I'm going to call them.' She pulled out her bright yellow cell phone and dialed.

'Going to DeVere isn't the only similarity between the victims,' Adam said, lowering his voice as Dani launched into a conversation on her cell. 'Dominic and Scott were both V. You know my theory about this.'

Jason nodded grimly. Suddenly Adam's vampire-hunter theory didn't seem so off the wall. What were the chances that a serial killer had accidentally chosen two vampires as his victims? 'OK, maybe you have a point,' Jason said quietly. 'But that still doesn't explain the attack on me.'

Adam shrugged. 'You were a mistake.'

Dani flipped her cell phone shut. 'I'm gonna go get in Maria's car,' she announced, taking off her seat belt. 'Kristy says we can all go to her house and study since school is closed.'

'Study what? The best fashions for a formal masked ball?' Jason teased her.

'Maybe.' Dani shot him a smile and climbed out of the Bug. He watched her run along the line of cars, waving to a few people she knew. Finally she climbed into Maria's Land Rover, which was next in line to make a U-turn in the high school's wide driveway. Jason waved as they turned around and headed the other way on the divided highway, then inched his car up a little bit as the line moved forwards.

Adam kept pace with him on the Vespa.

'Does Tamburo have any leads on the Challon case?' Jason asked.

'Not a one,' Adam replied. 'And my dad says Tamburo was on the scene within minutes of the attack. Between you and me, I think he's getting desperate.'

Jason moved the car up farther in the line. 'If it's a vampire hunter, that means the other vampires are in danger, too,' he said thoughtfully.

'Yup, it means Sienna is in danger,' Adam agreed.

'I didn't say Sienna,' Jason protested.

'But you were thinking it.' Adam revved the Vespa like it was a Harley Davidson. 'You're next for the U-turn, my friend. Wanna hit Eddie's for a breakfast burrito?'

'Sure. I'll meet you there.' Jason had reached the school gates, where a cop was directing traffic. As he drove the Bug through the circular driveway, he caught a glimpse of a few police officers roaming the grounds. He wondered what they could possibly be looking for. The killer wasn't a student, was he?

Then Jason was back out on Pacific Coast Highway, heading for Eddie's. And he wasn't the only one. By the time he got there, the small restaurant was packed with kids from school. Jason found a parking spot and headed inside to snag a table while waiting for Adam. He was hoping Sienna might be among the crowd; it wouldn't hurt to give her a heads up about the possibility of a vampire hunter, and it wouldn't hurt just to see her face, either. Any Sienna time was good Sienna time.

Except when she was surrounded by people who didn't like him.

Like Zach and Van Dyke, who were sitting on either side of Sienna at one of the small tables near the window. Erin sat across from them, completely blocking Jason's access to Sienna. He'd been meaning to pull her aside to tell her Adam's theory, but that was impossible now.

And a quick scan of the room showed him that the only table open was the one right next to the vampires.

'Great,' he muttered. Van Dyke had been giving him the cold shoulder for days, and Zach was never particularly friendly. He didn't feel like being anywhere near them right now. But it didn't look as if there was much choice. Squaring his shoulders, Jason went over and sat down. He caught Sienna's eye and nodded hello.

'Hi, guys,' Jason said, including the whole table in his greeting. He didn't want to make a big show of singling out Sienna.

'Hey, Jason,' Erin said. The guys didn't answer, and Sienna just gave him a little wave.

Mercifully, Adam showed up at that moment, barreling over to join Jason at the table. 'Excellent work,' he said. 'Ocean view and everything.'

'Oh, yeah.' Jason hadn't even bothered to look out of

the window. He'd been too busy trying not to stare at Sienna. He flipped open his menu and studied it.

'. . . body was still warm when the cops arrived,' Van Dyke was saying. 'The killer must've just left.'

'You'd think they could find him, then,' Erin said.

'It's not like he was right there, though,' Zach put in. 'He could shoot the crossbow bolt from a distance. He was probably a mile away before the police showed up.'

'Funny how I keep hearing the same conversation everywhere I go,' Adam said to Jason. 'My dad and the other cops, all the kids at this place. Everyone's trying to figure out who this killer is and why they can't find him.'

'But you think you know the answer,' Jason said.

'Well, not really. I don't know *who* he is. I just think I know *what* he is,' Adam replied. 'Although I haven't mentioned my theory to Detective Tamburo.'

'Maybe you should mention it to *them*,' Jason said, gesturing to the vampires' table. 'If you're right, they're in danger. And I don't think they have a clue.'

'I'm on it.' Adam yanked his chair closer to Erin's, making the metal legs screech against the stone floor. 'So listen, *amigos*,' he said, interrupting the vampires' conversation. 'Have you guys considered the fact that this killer might just be after . . . special people?'

Zach, Van Dyke, and Erin stared at him blankly. Sienna smiled a little.

'I'm sorry?' Zach said politely.

'This crossbow-carrying freak might be deliberately hunting certain types of people,' Adam said. 'You know, beautiful people. *Special* people.' When they continued to look confused, he rolled his eyes. '*Dentally-enhanced* people.'

Sienna's eyes widened, and Erin and Van Dyke laughed.

Jason was surprised that Adam was being so blunt about the whole thing. As far as he knew, Adam had never admitted to any of the vampires that he knew the truth about them. And yet here he was going head to head with Zach himself.

Zach stared at Adam for a long moment. Jason thought he looked as if he was trying not to laugh.

'I'm trying to help you,' Adam said. 'You need to be careful. I think this killer could be a . . . hunter.' He lowered his voice. 'A *vampire* hunter.'

Jason searched their faces, expecting to see alarm. Instead, Erin and Van Dyke rolled their eyes and grinned. Sienna chuckled and even Zach smiled.

'Well, we, er, appreciate your concern,' Zach said. 'But you've got this one wrong. There's no such thing as a vampire hunter.'

Sienna leaned forward. 'Er, there's no such thing as Santa either, Adam. I'm sorry to break it to you,' she teased.

'Santa's overrated anyway,' Adam quipped back. 'But you know, most people think there's no such thing as vampires. And they're wrong.'

'But if the *vampires* say there's no such thing as a vampire hunter, you might want to believe them,' Zach pointed out.

'OK,' Adam replied, unconvinced. 'But somebody has managed to kill two of you in less than a week. I'm just sayin'.'

'Two vampires. Two DeVere Heights students. Two guys who were both into Green Day. Who knows why Dominic and Scott were both targeted?' Van Dyke put in. 'But I can tell you it wasn't because of some medieval vampire-hunter guy.'

'I don't think they existed even then,' Erin said. 'I think they were always a myth.'

Adam shot Jason a can-you-believe-this look, and Jason shrugged. One thing he'd learned since moving to Malibu was not to get involved in too much vampire stuff. Every time he'd got pulled in, it had meant only one thing – trouble.

'Relax. You've given them a heads up. I guess these guys can take care of themselves now,' he told Adam.

'True.' Zach gave Jason the smallest of smiles. Then he stood up. 'Let's go, Van Dyke. We're late to meet Brad.'

Immediately a chill fell over the table. Jason felt like everybody was looking at him – and at Sienna – to see how they responded to the mention of Brad. He did his best not to change the expression on his face, but he felt a flush creeping up his neck. Did every single person they knew think that he and Sienna were having a thing?

Van Dyke stood up and made a big show of saying goodbye to everyone except Jason. Once he and Zach were gone, Erin turned to Sienna with her eyebrows raised. 'Adam and I can leave, too, if you guys want to be alone,' she teased.

'No!' Sienna said quickly.

'Nuh-uh,' Jason replied at the same time.

Their eyes met and they both laughed.

'We're friends,' Sienna said. 'That's all. Right, Jason?'

'Right,' he confirmed.

'Right,' Erin said, a tinge of sarcasm in her voice. 'How's the weather there in Denial Land?' she murmured, but she was smiling.

Adam tried not to laugh.

Jason decided to ignore them. But Sienna was embarrassed. 'Actually, I better go, too,' she said. 'I have to pick up the place cards from the calligrapher.'

'Place cards?' Jason queried.

'Yes. For the masked ball,' Sienna explained.

'That's not still going ahead, is it?' Jason asked in disbelief.

'Are you kidding?' It was Erin's turn to sound incredulous. 'Of course it is.'

'I just thought, with another murder . . .' Jason let his sentence trail off.

'Important people are coming from all over to go to the ball. They've spent a lot of money on the tickets. And it's all for charity. We can't just cancel it,' Sienna explained.

'That's true, I guess,' Jason said, realizing he still had a lot to learn about the Malibu way of thinking.

'You're still coming, aren't you?' Sienna asked, sounding just the slightest bit anxious.

'Of course I am,' Jason replied. 'We all need something to cheer us up, and the ball will probably do the trick.' *And besides*, Jason thought, *would I miss seeing Sienna in her element? Not a chance.*

ELEVEN

After school on Tuesday, Jason headed straight for the pool. One day off of swim practice was enough. He had to be there to support the team because, hey, he was on the team, and he wasn't going to let Brad and Van Dyke edge him out.

'Jason!' Dani's voice echoed through the emptying hallway. 'Wait up!'

He turned to see his sister jogging toward him, her auburn hair swinging wildly.

'I can't drive you home until later,' he told her when she reached him. 'I'm going to practice.'

'I don't need a ride. I just wanted to ask you a favor,' she said breathlessly. 'I'm going shopping with Kristy for a dress.'

'OK. So what's the favor?'

'I need you to back me up tonight at dinner,' Dani said. 'Kristy's parents gave her a budget of seven hundred dollars.'

'For what?'

'The *dress*,' Dani said impatiently. 'And I know Mom and Dad are gonna flip when I ask for that much. So you have to help me convince them.'

Jason whistled. 'Where are you going to shop? The Diamond-studded Dress Store?'

'I'm not saying I'll spend that much. I'm just saying that if I find the perfect dress and it's as expensive as Kristy's, I want to be able to buy it.' Dani crossed her arms over her chest, a sure sign she was going to be stubborn about this. 'I mean, Dad makes tons of money now. So what's a few hundred bucks—'

'Seven hundred.'

'OK, seven hundred bucks to him?' Dani went on. 'Besides, it's important. Sunday night is a big romance night for me, astrologically speaking. I have to look my best.'

'There is absolutely no way Mom will ever let you buy a dress that expensive,' Jason said. 'Whether I back you up or not.'

'Please?' Dani begged. 'She listens to you more than me. She thinks you're the responsible one.'

'I *am* the responsible one,' Jason said.

'So you have to help me.' Dani smiled brightly.

'I'll think about it,' Jason promised. 'But right now I

have to get to practice.' He gave her a wave and headed off toward the locker room.

As soon as he stepped inside, he could feel the tension in the air. Nobody was worried about how to dress for the charity ball here, they were all too busy worrying about the psycho crossbow killer.

'... Tamburo obviously thinks it's somebody we know,' Harberts was saying. 'He interviewed me again today.'

'Maybe he suspects you,' Priesmeyer said. Jason knew he was joking, but there was an edge to his voice.

'Well, I know I didn't do it.' Harberts slammed his locker shut. 'But there have to be some clues that are leading to a student at DeVere. Why else would the cops be focusing the investigation here?'

Jason kept quiet. If he didn't say anything, there was less of a chance that his team mates would ignore him. Or at least, if they were ignoring him, he wouldn't have to have it rubbed in his face. Brad wasn't here yet, but Van Dyke was digging through his locker right next to Harberts.

'I think it's TJ Warwick,' Van Dyke said. 'He always hated Dominic. Remember when Dom beat him up in ninth grade?'

'Dominic beat everybody up,' Harberts replied.

'That was his favorite thing to do. He even tried to beat up Jason, remember? And even if TJ hated Dominic, why would he go after Scott?'

'Yeah. It doesn't make sense,' Priesmeyer said. 'There's no point in all of us turning on each other, it will just make everybody paranoid.'

The door swung open, and Brad walked in. Jason made a beeline for him, leaving the other guys to speculate about potential murderers they went to school with.

'Hey, Brad,' Jason said, intercepting him near the doorway. 'Listen, I wanted to tell you I'm sorry to hear about you and Sienna—'

'Oh, please,' Brad interrupted. 'You didn't get enough of a kick from going behind my back with Sienna? Now you're going to lie to my face?'

'I'm not lying,' Jason protested. 'And I didn't go behind your back with Sienna.'

'Freeman, you've been after Sienna since the first time you saw her,' Brad spat. 'You think I'm stupid? Well, now you've got her. Congratulations.'

'I don't have her. I'm not with her,' Jason insisted. 'I'm not denying she's beautiful, but—'

'Curt!' Brad cried suddenly, cutting Jason off mid-sentence. 'You made it!'

Jason turned to see a tall African-American guy, who seemed to be made entirely of muscle, slapping hands with Brad.

'Yeah, and you owe me big time,' Curt said with a grin. 'Don't think I like leaving my own school in the middle of the year to help out your sorry butt.'

Brad clapped him on the shoulder and turned him toward the other guys on the team, leaving Jason alone by the door. 'Everyone, listen up,' Brad called. 'This is Curt Tungsten from Santa Monica. He's agreed to come live at my house for the rest of the season so he can go to school here and, more importantly, help us out on relay.'

'Teach you the meaning of the word relay, you mean,' Curt joked.

'He's our new Jason,' Brad said loudly. 'And he's got an even better record than the old one!'

Jason watched numbly as Brad introduced Curt to the rest of the guys. Clearly, nothing he could do was going to restore his friendship with Brad. He decided he was just going to have to take it on the chin.

After Curt had met everyone, he went over to an empty locker to change.

Jason wandered over to him. 'I hear you're the new Jason,' he said, extending his hand. 'I'm the old Jason.'

'Oh. Whoops,' Curt said, shaking Jason's hand. 'Sorry about that. It's just trash talk. From what I hear, you're pretty irreplaceable.'

'I doubt that,' Jason said easily. 'But thanks for saying so. You're taking over my place on relay. Make me proud.'

'Will do.' Curt nodded at him and headed through the swinging door to the pool. Jason sighed and wondered whether he was ever going to get his normal life back?

'I'll be the only one there in a stupid fifty-dollar cocktail dress!' Dani's voice carried up from downstairs as Jason sat down at his computer on Thursday evening.

'You're going to be wearing a mask, aren't you?' his mother replied. 'So no one will be able to tell that you're the "crazy" one who didn't spend a fortune on a dress she would wear for exactly five hours.'

'It's not funny,' Dani protested.

It is a little bit funny, Jason thought. As predicted, his mom had refused to let Danielle spend hundreds of dollars on a dress for Sienna's charity ball. And Dani was convinced that if she didn't have an expensive dress, the guy she was hoping to meet wouldn't even notice her. Jason had pointed out that if it were truly in the stars, the guy wouldn't care what she was wearing, but Dani had just rolled her eyes.

Jason shut his door to block out the ongoing argument downstairs. He had to get some homework done. He flipped open his history notebook and glanced over the assignment for the next week's current-events essay. Everyone in his class was supposed to write about a local zoning-board issue – as if studying something so boring would distract them from the fact that a serial killer was picking off their classmates. *That* was the only current event he – or anyone else – really cared about right now.

With a sigh, he opened his internet browser and called up the Malibu city council website. Just as he was clicking on the zoning-laws page, his computer gave a little bell tone and an instant message window popped up. Jason quickly opened it – maybe it was Tyler finally checking in. But a glance at the screen name and message made Jason forget all about Tyler for the moment.

BadGirlDev: Michigan?

It was Sienna. It had to be. They had never talked on IM before, but obviously she'd managed to find his screen name. Jason hit reply and began to type:

MalibuFreeman: I don't know if I should be answering IM from a bad girl.

BadGirlDev: Why? Do I scare U?

MalibuFreeman: A little. ☺

BadGirlDev: Intelligent women are intimidating!

MalibuFreeman: Intelligent, beautiful women are downright terrifying.

There was a pause. Jason stared at the message window, wondering if he'd gone too far. He wasn't supposed to be flirting with Sienna. They were just friends. You didn't go around telling your friends they were beautiful. Maybe he'd freaked her out. But he didn't want to leave it like that. He quickly typed another message:

MalibuFreeman: How'd U know my screen name? Were U searching for me?

BadGirlDev: Not many Freemans in Malibu. U & Dani.

MalibuFreeman: U were totally searching for me.

BadGirlDev: Maybe I wanted Dani.

MalibuFreeman: 4 what?

BadGirlDev: Umm . . .

MalibuFreeman: :D

Jason sat back, grinning. He'd caught her – she'd been looking for him. Did that mean she sat around thinking about him the way he did about her?

BadGirlDev: School was weird today. Depressing.

MalibuFreeman: I know. Everyone's paranoid.

He couldn't help thinking about the crossbow-killer conversation in the locker room as he typed. His friends on the team were certainly getting paranoid – if he could still call them his friends. He wasn't sure anymore, what with the way they'd all welcomed Curt so warmly. Was he being replaced permanently? It was starting to seem like Brad would never forgive him.

He noticed that Sienna had written more while he was thinking.

BadGirlDev: What R U doing?

MalibuFreeman: Homework. U?

BadGirlDev: Shopping for a Venetian mask. I want a sexy one for the ball.

MalibuFreeman: Like what?

BadGirlDev: Cat's-eye, maybe. Or one with jewels that hang on my forehead. Or long feathers.

MalibuFreeman: Go for feathers.

BadGirlDev: Y?

MalibuFreeman: They're good for tickling.

BadGirlDev: Sounds like fun.

Jason sat back, smiling. Somehow the idea of Sienna in a mask made her seem even more mysterious and exotic than usual – and that was saying something. But even with a mask covering her face, Jason was certain that he'd still recognize her lips and her deep brown eyes . . .

Another soft bell tone woke him from his daydream. A new IM window had opened on top of Sienna's. This time it was Adam.

CineGeek: Yo, homey, what up?

Jason smiled. Adam had terrible timing, but maybe it was a good thing. If he kept IM-ing with Sienna, things might get out of hand. He was supposed to be playing things cool with her. So maybe taking a break for a few minutes would help. He hit reply to answer Adam.

MalibuFreeman: Not much. Doing research.

CineGeek: Me too. Check it:

A link popped up in the window, so Jason clicked on it. Immediately a giant picture of a mouth appeared on screen – a mouth with two gleaming, razor-sharp fangs. As he watched, a drop of bright red blood appeared and dripped from one of the fangs, oozing out into a red blob that expanded to fill the whole screen. A word in black appeared over the red:

Vampyre!

Jason shook his head. Leave it to Adam!

MalibuFreeman: Cheesy.

CineGeek: Cheesy & password protected. Luckily I

can hack. Only took an hour to break into the site! Take a look.

MalibuFreeman: I'm looking at zoning laws.

CineGeek: Well, stop it. The vampyre site is much more interesting, believe me.

Jason clicked back to the vampyre site. The intro page had been replaced by a menu that appeared to be written in blood. And at the top of the list of contents was something called 'Hunters of the Undead'. Obviously that was what Adam wanted him to see. He opened the page.

The first thing he saw were about ten different pictures of crossbows. The article that accompanied the photos was entitled 'Modern Hunters, Traditional Weapons'. A quick scan of it told Jason all he needed to know – that these days, vampire hunters liked to track their prey through bank accounts and internet research. But apparently they still liked to kill the vampires the old-fashioned way, with a crossbow bolt to the heart before the full moon.

Jason's chest ached where the metal arrow had embedded itself. Just looking at the photos was enough to remind him of the pain. And suddenly a new image of Sienna appeared in his mind: Sienna in her evening gown, lowering her mask and smiling at him, looking impossibly beautiful, until a metal bolt flew through the air and impaled her. Piercing her heart.

Killing her.

Fear shot through Jason. He had to convince Sienna that Adam was right about the vampire hunter. He had to make her see that she was in danger. He closed the vampyre page and went back to Sienna's IM window. He was no longer interested in playing it cool.

MalibuFreeman: Sienna, Adam's right. There's a vampire hunter.

A window popped up in response: *Username BadGirlDev not currently signed on.*

Jason sighed. That was typical of Sienna, he thought, around just long enough to intrigue him, and then gone. But perhaps it was just as well. Things had been getting a little too heated between them and he had to cool it down.

Besides, he had other things to think about. He was more worried than ever about the possibility of a vampire hunter. Were more vampires going to die before the moon was full? And was there anything he could do to stop it?

TWELVE

'Tell me again why we're voluntarily subjecting our-selves to this?' Adam said on Saturday evening. He gestured toward the backseat of the VW, where Dani and Kristy were sitting. They were in high spirits since it had been announced the previous day at school that the curfew would indeed be lifted for the night of the masked ball. The girls had been talking about clothes non-stop since Jason had pulled out of the driveway in Malibu.

But that discussion didn't stop Dani from overhear-ing Jason and Adam's conversation. 'Because you two need to get out of the house and live a little,' she replied. 'It's the weekend. Time for fun. Whatever fun we can squeeze in before curfew tonight.'

'Shockingly, we don't necessarily think an in-depth analysis of Eva Longoria's premiere outfit is fun,' Jason joked.

Dani playfully stuck her tongue out at him. 'Fine.

What do you want to talk about?'

'Who cares? We're here,' Kristy put in.

Jason pulled the car into the parking lot near the Santa Monica Pier. Once he'd stopped, the girls climbed out and rushed toward the brightly lit boardwalk. Jason and Adam followed more slowly. Jason had to admit that he was happy Dani had convinced him to come out tonight. He'd been on edge for the last couple of days, wondering if another tragedy was coming and racking his brains for anything he could remember or think of that might help the police catch the killer before he could strike again. Until the vampire-hunting season ended, Jason just wasn't going to feel comfortable. But the pier was always fun, like a permanent carnival on the beach, and he figured it would help to take his mind off things.

'I can name at least ten movies that have been shot here,' Adam commented as they all climbed the weathered wooden stairs up to the pier. 'Starting with—'

'Ooh! A fortune-telling machine!' Dani cried, interrupting him. She grabbed Kristy's arm and tugged her toward the old-fashioned machine which had a little model genie in a turban inside.

'Coming, Jason?' Dani called over her shoulder.

'Maybe it will tell you whether you've got a Devereux in your future.'

Jason was just opening his mouth to protest when Adam nudged him. 'You don't need a machine to tell you that,' he said. 'Look.'

Sure enough, Sienna was standing ten feet away, waiting as Erin and Maggie bought ice-cream cones from a shop along the boardwalk. Jason felt a tingle dance along his spine at the sight of her.

As if she'd felt his eyes on her, Sienna turned around. When she saw him, a slow smile spread across her face.

'Here we go,' Adam murmured, mock-hurt. 'Sienna shows up and that's it for our guys' night out.'

'We weren't having a guys' night out,' Jason reminded him.

'Oh. Right. Well, in that case, let's go hang with the three scorching babes,' Adam said, trotting cheerfully over to Sienna and her crew. 'Ladies! What's the what?' he cried.

'Adam! Just the man I wanted to see,' Maggie declared.

'Really?' Adam was so surprised that he stopped walking. Jason chuckled and shoved him forward a few steps.

'Yeah. You must have some inside info on the killer,' Maggie said. 'Does your father think they're close to arresting anybody? Because my parents are threatening to send me to boarding school if they don't catch the guy soon.'

'Seriously. Van Dyke's mom is organizing a big meeting for all the parental units on Monday,' Erin put in. 'They're thinking of hiring a private investigator because the police aren't getting the job done.' She glanced at Adam. 'Sorry.'

'I don't think a P.I. is going to help,' Adam replied. 'They won't find anybody better than Tamburo.'

'I agree,' Jason said. 'The guy's relentless. He'll find the killer.' Although, secretly, he was beginning to wonder. If Adam's theory was right and the killer was a vampire hunter, then Tamburo was operating without all the relevant information. He didn't understand the link between the victims. Well, between two of the victims. And if the killer had seen Jason buying back the chalice, he would probably have thought that Jason was a vampire too.

'You're looking pensive,' Sienna said, stepping up next to him.

Jason jumped, surprised. He hadn't realized how long he'd been standing there, mulling over the vampire-hunter situation. Adam and the other girls had already started walking up the pier, still discussing the case.

'Yeah. I'm worried about this killer,' he admitted. 'I'm pretty much on board with Adam's theory—'

'I don't want to talk about it,' Sienna said quickly, and Jason could see an edgy, uneasy light in her eyes. 'I just can't stand any more murder talk. Every single word out of everybody's mouth lately is about this killer, and it's making me crazy.'

'But—'

'I'm not going to listen to you if you talk about it,' she said seriously, putting her finger to his lips.

Jason nodded. Maybe it was better not to freak Sienna out anymore than she already was.

'Good,' Sienna said and gave him a lingering smile. 'Let's catch up to the others. They're going to the amusement park.'

'Hang on,' Jason said. He raced over to Dani and Kristy at the fortune-telling machine. 'We ran into some friends, and we're going to head over to the rides with them.'

Dani stood on tiptoes to look over his shoulder. 'Some friends? Looks more like Sienna to me.' She raised an eyebrow and grinned at him.

Jason ignored her skeptical expression. 'Anyway, I'll meet you back here in an hour, OK?'

'Have fun,' Dani called after him as he jogged back over to Sienna.

'Sorry if I cut you off a minute ago,' she said as they walked toward the gateway that led to the small amusement park that ran along one side of the pier. 'I'm just so sick of discussing the murders. Do you know, I had a reporter ask me about it today?'

'You make a habit of talking to the press?' he teased.

'No.' Sienna slapped his arm. 'My mom was doing an interview for the society section in the *Times*, and I was just sitting in. It was supposed to be about the charity ball, but the guy just kept asking me questions about the murders: Did I know the victims? How were kids at school dealing with it? All that garbage.'

'Hey, lovebirds, hurry up!' Adam called from the ticket booth. 'It's time for Whack-a-mole.'

Sienna shot Jason a smile. 'I'm really good at Whack-a-mole,' she warned him. 'So don't think you're going to be beating me.'

'Are you kidding?' he cried. 'Girls can't whack with nearly the strength required to be a true Whack-a-mole master.'

'Oh, you are so going down.' Sienna walked over to

the Whack-a-mole booth and slapped down a dollar. 'I'm going to kick this guy's butt,' she told the tattoo-covered guy behind the counter.

'Good for you,' he replied with a grin.

Jason laughed and coughed up a buck of his own. Then he and Sienna both grabbed big padded mallets and waited for the little mechanical moles to begin popping up.

'I have a feeling this is going to get ugly,' Adam joked. 'I think I'll wait for the next round.'

A buzzer sounded, the moles began to pop, and they both started slamming the mallets down at the little critters.

Jason hit three.

Sienna hit nine.

'The lady wins by a landslide,' Tattoo Guy yelled when they'd finished. 'You get a stuffed animal,' he told Sienna.

She turned to Jason, her face flushed with laughter. 'What do you want?' she asked in a teasing voice.

'Ooohhh,' Maggie and Erin cried.

'You know, Jason, it's supposed to be the other way around,' Adam said. 'You win the prize for the girl.'

'You think I'm going to turn down a free stuffed

toy?' Jason asked. 'No way. I want the snake,' he told Sienna.

She laughed and turned to Tattoo Guy. 'The snake it is.' He handed over the silly-looking purple snake and Sienna presented it to Jason.

'Thanks,' he said. 'But I'll totally beat you in the fake bowling game.'

'Bring it on,' she said. 'I'm the queen of every stupid amusement-park game there is.'

'Forget about the game-booth war,' Adam put in. 'Let's go on the Ferris wheel.'

Erin and Maggie immediately set off for the giant wheel, and Adam hurried after them.

Jason caught Sienna's eye, and they both laughed. 'I could use a ride on the Ferris wheel,' she said. 'Whenever I need a little perspective, I come here. When you're way at the top, the whole world looks tiny and all your problems seem small, too.'

'Then what are we waiting for?' Jason said. 'Let's go ride on the problem-shrinker.'

Sienna reached for his hand, then stopped. She blushed and quickly looked away. 'OK, let's go,' she murmured, heading for the ticket booth.

She didn't look at him again during the wait to buy tickets, or the walk through the crowded park. But

Jason felt like he was flying the whole time. She'd almost taken his hand! As if they were together, boyfriend and girlfriend, and it had seemed so natural that she hadn't even realized she was doing it until the last second.

Soon it was their turn to board the Ferris wheel. The thing was huge, at least nine stories high, and the cars weren't your usual rinky-dink two seaters. They were like small tram cars, and each one held six people.

Adam jumped up to the car at the bottom of the wheel, opened the little door, and gestured Maggie and Erin inside. 'After you, ladies,' he said. Once they were in, he hopped in after them, yanked the door shut, and grinned at Jason. 'Sorry, we're full,' he lied.

'Yeah, you guys will have to go in the next one,' Erin called. She and Maggie giggled as the wheel began to move and their cart was lifted up into the air, leaving Jason and Sienna all alone.

Now she had no choice. She had to look at him.

They gazed at each other in silence for a moment. 'They're so rude,' Sienna said finally, breaking the tension.

Jason laughed. 'That's all right. We're tough. We can handle a ride by ourselves.' He opened the door and they climbed in. Sienna sat on the bench to the right, so he moved to sit across from her.

'Get over here,' Sienna ordered playfully. 'I can barely even see you all the way on the other side of the car. You're like eight feet away from me.'

'It's more like three feet.' But he got up and moved to sit beside her. He'd just managed to get his butt in the seat when the ride began to move.

'It will take at least ten minutes to get the whole wheel loaded with people,' Sienna said as they jerked to a stop a few seconds later.

'I guess we have some time then,' Jason said, wondering what to do with his hands. He was sitting so close to Sienna now that their thighs were pressed lightly together. The obvious thing to do was to put his arm around her. But he couldn't. They were just friends. And even though Brad wanted nothing to do with him, Jason still considered *him* a friend, as well. It was too soon to make a move on Brad's ex. As long as Brad still had feelings for Sienna, Jason felt that she was off-limits to him.

The ride moved again, pulling them another few feet into the air before it stopped. Neither of them had said anything in a while, and Jason was starting to feel awkward. 'So how's Belle doing?' he asked.

'Not too good,' Sienna said softly. 'I called her cell tonight, but she didn't answer. I doubt she would have felt up to coming out, anyway. She's still really upset about Dominic. It's hard to believe he's gone. You just take things for granted, you know? Like that Belle and Dominic would always be together. They'd go to the prom together, head off to the same college, all that stuff.'

She paused, and Jason took a deep breath. He wasn't sure he should say anything about Brad, but he felt he had to. 'You probably felt that way about you and Brad, too,' he said gently. 'That you'd go to the prom, and go to college together.'

'Yeah. I guess I did.' Sienna turned to face him. 'But the truth is, I was just taking that for granted. I didn't necessarily want it anymore. I mean, I love Brad. But I'm not *in* love with him. Not now.'

Jason didn't answer. What was there to say? He couldn't exactly ask whether she'd stopped loving her boyfriend because of him, and it really wasn't any of his business.

'I think I started having second thoughts about Brad around the time school started this year,' Sienna went on, and she looked up at Jason briefly, *meaningfully*.

Jason leaned back against the seat, his heart racing.

He'd first met Sienna at the beginning of the school year. So she'd basically answered the question he'd been wanting to ask. But Jason felt powerless to do anything with that information. Brad was still cut up about Sienna and mad at Jason, and apparently with good reason. Jason hadn't intended to steal the guy's girlfriend, but still . . .

'Brad's a great guy,' he said carefully. 'He was the first one on the swim team to make friends with me.'

'Yeah. He's the best,' Sienna agreed. 'The last thing I would ever want to do is hurt him.'

'Me either.' Jason was glad that Sienna seemed to understand what he was saying.

'I think he'll realize I was right about us, that we weren't really in love anymore,' Sienna said. 'But he needs some time.'

'Right. It's not like you could run right out and start dating someone else,' Jason replied.

'Exactly,' Sienna said, her face lighting up in a huge smile. The ride took them higher still, and then their car jerked to a stop at the very top of the Ferris wheel. 'I think I can start seeing someone else one of these days,' she went on. 'Just not right away.'

Jason nodded. 'Sure.'

They sat quietly for a moment, gazing out at the

view – the dark ocean to one side, the brightly lit pier to the other. Jason knew they'd reached an understanding. Without ever really saying so, they'd agreed that they couldn't be together yet. They had to wait for a while, out of respect for Brad.

But that still meant that he and Sienna could be together someday. And that was enough. For now.

'You're right about the Ferris wheel,' he told her, smiling. 'Problems seem smaller up here.'

'And beautiful things seem bigger,' Sienna replied with an answering smile. 'Look at the moon. Isn't it gorgeous?'

Jason glanced at the full moon, hanging low over the horizon. From where they sat, the moon appeared to take up half the sky. But his eyes immediately returned to Sienna. The silvery light danced over her silky hair, and her face seemed to glow. 'You're gorgeous,' he said softly.

Sienna gazed into his eyes, and Jason found himself even closer to her. Close enough to brush his lips against hers . . .

The Ferris wheel gave a jerk, and Jason fell away from Sienna. He gave a rueful laugh as the ride began in earnest. Their car whizzed down the other side and began to climb smoothly back up again.

Concentrate on the ride, Jason ordered himself. *No kissing Sienna.*

Not yet.

'You missed a spot,' Jason told his sister the next morning. 'On the left side of the windshield.'

Dani dropped her soapy sponge into the bucket and frowned at him. 'You're pushing it, big brother,' she replied. 'You know I don't think this counts as one of your chores to begin with.'

'Well, the car doesn't wash itself,' he said, grinning as he took another swig of his Coke and relaxed in the cushy porch swing near the front door. 'And you use it, too, sort of.'

'Yeah, yeah,' Dani grumbled. She squeezed out the sponge and soaped up the windshield again. 'But I don't know why you have to watch me.'

'I'm supervising,' Jason said. 'You'd never do it right otherwise.'

'You're not *supervising*, you're *torturing*.' She flicked some suds at him. 'Go away!'

'Oh, all right. I guess you can handle the rinse yourself.' Jason stood up and stretched. He was just pulling open the front door when he heard the beeping of a horn. He turned to see Adam pulling into the driveway on his Vespa.

'Freeman!' Adam yelled. He motored past Dani, hopped off the bike, grabbed Jason's arm and dragged him inside. 'I have news. They haven't released it to the public yet, but I had to come and tell you.' He took a deep breath and then spoke in a more serious tone than Jason had ever heard him use before. 'There's been another murder.'

THIRTEEN

'Who was it?' Jason demanded, his heart pounding with fear. Had one of his friends been killed? Was it Sienna?

'Trinny Dareau,' Adam replied. 'She was killed this morning. It was another crossbow-bolt murder. You've seen her. She's a cheerleader in your sister's year.'

Jason nodded, relaxing a little. It was horrible that a girl had been killed, but he couldn't help feeling relieved that it was nobody he knew. 'She's got red hair, right?'

'No.'

'Oh. Well, her name sounds familiar anyway,' Jason said.

'Yeah.' Adam headed for the stairs. 'Let's go up to your room.'

'OK.' Jason followed him up and closed his bedroom door behind them. 'What's up?'

'It's Trinny,' Adam said seriously. 'She wasn't a vampire.'

Jason dropped down into his desk chair. 'And they're sure it was the same killer?'

'According to Tamburo, it's the exact same M.O.' Adam paced up and down the room. 'Except for the fact that Trinny was human.'

Jason sighed. 'But that doesn't make sense,' he said.

Adam nodded. 'Looks like my vampire-hunter theory was wrong.'

'Yeah, I guess,' Jason said slowly. He could hardly believe it. Adam's theory had really grown on him. He'd been sure it was true. 'So the theory is wrong,' Jason repeated, drumming his fingers on the desk thoughtfully. 'That means that the killer's just a nut job, like Tamburo said.'

'Yeah. I feel stupid for doing all that research on hunters,' Adam said. 'Zach told me there was no such thing. I should've believed him.'

'You were only trying to help,' Jason said. 'And at least you had a theory. Does Tamburo have one? Does he have *any* idea who's doing this, or why?'

'I don't think so. He knows it's the same killer, because the bolts from the crossbow are very specific,' Adam said. 'Tamburo had the forensics guys check out the bolt that killed Trinny. It's got a groove in the same place as the bolts that hit you, Dominic and Scott. The groove is made by an uneven piece of metal on the crossbow he uses.'

'But that's all? He doesn't even have a suspect?' Jason asked.

'Unfortunately, no. But my dad says he's handling the case as well as it can be handled.' Adam frowned. 'I think it's just that without anything linking the victims, it's impossible to figure out what the motive is.'

'I wasn't thrilled to think that all the vampires were in danger. But I'm less thrilled now,' Jason said thoughtfully. 'Because if the killer isn't targeting vampires, then everyone is in danger. And the guy is also that much harder to catch. If he's after random people, and we have no idea what his motive is, he could go after anyone.'

'At any time,' Adam agreed. 'If it were a vampire hunter, the season would be over after tonight – at least until the next new moon and the next hunting season starts. But now we'll have to keep worrying. There's no end in sight.'

Jason sighed. 'It's useless to sit around thinking about it. Tamburo's a hotshot. He'll find the killer sooner or later. We just *have* to trust him to do his job.'

'I guess so.' Adam cracked a smile. 'And my dad was right to bring him in. Around here, the worst the regular cops usually have to deal with is credit-card fraud. At least Tamburo has actually caught murderers before.'

Jason stood up. 'I'm going to head out back and do a few exercises in the pool,' he said. 'I'm not allowed to swim, but I can use the water for resistance training. I need to start getting myself back in shape.'

'I'll come along and stick my feet in the water,' Adam said. 'Those of us without luxurious heated pools have to pounce on any opportunity we get.'

Jason led the way downstairs and out to the backyard.

'You're a glutton for punishment,' Adam commented. 'I saw you driving to the pier last night, wincing every time you had to turn the steering wheel. You're still in pain.'

'I need to keep my muscles in shape for when I can actually swim again,' Jason told him. 'And I'm only in a little pain now.'

'Yeah, but if I were in even a little bit of pain, I would use it as an excuse to sit around eating Fritos and channel surfing,' Adam said. 'But you, Mr Overachiever, *you* have to get back in shape before your wound is even healed!'

'Oh, please,' Danielle said, carrying the car-wash

bucket over to the storage shed near the pool. 'Jason just wants to impress Sienna with his rippling muscles at the charity ball tonight.'

Adam laughed.

'Not true,' Jason said. 'And if you keep saying things like that, I'll tell everyone at the ball that your dress only cost fifty bucks!'

Dani gasped, shooting a mortified look at Adam.

'Hey, don't worry about me,' Adam told her. 'My tux is rented from Cheap Tuxes R Us.'

'It doesn't matter how much it cost, anyway. Billy helped me redesign the dress, so it's really an original couture design piece now,' Dani told him. 'And if Jason tells anyone else how much I spent on it, I might have to mention a little trip he took out to the desert. Because I don't think Sienna will find him so cool once I tell her about the Arcana Psychic Fair!'

Adam burst out laughing. 'I'm sorry. I didn't know I had a friend who's into the occult,' he teased. 'I thought I was supposed to be the wacky one. But even I draw the line at attending psychic gatherings.'

Dani winked at Jason as she put the bucket away.

'So what's your specialty?' Adam went on, mock-seriously. 'Astrology? Or are you more of a palm-reading type, dude? No, wait, don't tell me – you divine the future using tea leaves, right?'

Jason decided it was time for a subject change. 'I bet the ball isn't even happening tonight, is it?'

Dani paled. 'It's not? It has to! I'm supposed to meet the love of my life tonight! Why would the ball be cancelled?'

'Er, no reason. I'm just kidding,' Jason said quickly. He'd forgotten that the news about Trinny Dareau wasn't public knowledge yet.

'Don't joke about things like that,' Dani said. She disappeared back inside the house, and Jason turned to Adam.

'Is the ball cancelled?' he asked. 'I mean, three murders in a row – that's got to have everyone on edge.'

'Nope, it's going on as scheduled,' Adam said. 'My father is getting a lot of pressure from the Devereuxs not to cancel it. They've got all kinds of influential people coming from Bel Air and Beverly Hills.'

'Plus, if they cancel it, the charities it benefits won't get the money,' Jason said.

'And Tamburo told my dad it would be better to let the ball go ahead anyway,' Adam added. 'I know I've told you about Trinny, but don't tell anyone else; they want to keep her murder quiet. Tamburo thinks maybe the killer likes all the attention he's been getting lately. So if we don't give him any public attention for murdering Trinny . . .'

'Like by canceling the big ball,' Jason put in.

'Yeah,' Adam agreed. 'Well, then he might try to strike again in order to get noticed. And if he's acting in haste, he's more likely to mess up and do something stupid. You know, like try to attack someone in a crowded public place. Tamburo is hoping that he'll try to strike again at the ball itself.'

'That doesn't sound very good,' Jason said, alarmed.

'Don't worry, my dad's got every cop on the force working the ball,' Adam assured him. 'Some of them will be in uniform, and the rest plainclothes. The killer will avoid the uniforms, but he'll find it harder to spot the other cops.'

'And the plainclothes cops will catch him before he acts,' Jason guessed. 'I hope it works. The whole thing sounds risky to me. Innocent people could get hurt.'

'Well, Tamburo is a risk-taker. And he figures innocent people are already getting killed, so it's worth the risk if it means we can catch the guy.'

'And your father agrees?'

'Not exactly,' Adam said. 'He's just made sure that he's got enough people working the ball so that they'll catch the guy before he can hurt anyone.'

'It's probably a good idea either way,' Jason said. 'Tamburo obviously thinks the killer is somebody local. Even if he's not planning to attack tonight, he might be at the ball.' He headed toward the back door. 'In which case, I'd better get ready.'

'What? Why?' Adam asked, hurrying after him. 'I thought you were resistance training.'

'No time. I want to get there early,' Jason said.

'Why?' Adam asked. 'Did Sienna ask you to help set up?'

'No. I'm sure they've hired an army of people to do that,' Jason said. 'And that's the problem. If Tamburo is right and the killer comes to the ball tonight, it's possible that he may come as a worker, not a guest . . .'

'. . . so he could be there already,' Adam finished for him.

'Yeah. Which means that Sienna could be in danger,' Jason said grimly. 'She's already there, too.'

They went back upstairs to Jason's room. While Jason began putting on the tux his father had bought him for his cousin's wedding last year, Adam scanned Jason's CD collection. Jason grabbed a pair of cufflinks, barely stopping to check that they matched. Right now, he just wanted to get to the ball.

'It's weird, don't you think?' Adam asked. 'All the violent things that have been happening around here lately? First that rogue vampire. Then the DeVere Vampire Council sentencing your mate Tyler to death. And now somebody killing people, including a couple of vampires.'

'Yup. Lots of bad mojo,' Jason agreed. 'Which is ironic, considering how safe everybody always says Malibu is.'

'Hmm,' Adam murmured, staring out of the window.

Jason could tell his friend wasn't even listening. 'All right, Turnball, out with it,' he said. 'You've got your thoughtful detective look on.'

'It just seems like every strange thing that happens is about vampires. So why would this be any different?' Adam replied. 'Two of the victims were vampires. One is a vampire sympathizer . . .'

'Is that what I am?' Jason asked, amused.

'Yes. A guy who hangs with vampires and who could have been seen at a pawn shop retrieving vampire property,' Adam said. 'You're a vamp-esque kinda guy. And Trinny was French . . .'

'And French in Malibu usually equals vampire,' Jason put in, realizing what Adam meant.

'Exactly,' Adam agreed. 'If somebody was looking

for the fangy types around here, they'd assume anybody who happened to be of French descent was probably a vampire. I mean, even *we* thought Trinny was a vampire when we first found out that vampires existed. Remember? We put her on our final list of everybody who we thought might possibly be V.'

'That's right!' Jason cried. 'That's why her name sounded familiar.'

'Yeah, we wrote down every single French person in the school,' Adam said. 'I think I was a little bit vampire-obsessed back then.'

'A little bit?' Jason said skeptically. At the start of the school year, Adam had been on a quest to uncover the truth about the existence of vampires in Malibu. He and Jason had started writing down the names of vampire suspects. Then they'd ordered that list into a new, complete and alphabetical list, and then Adam had researched every single person on it.

'You know, I don't think I ever crossed Trinny off when we realized she wasn't a vampire,' Adam said slowly.

Jason felt a sudden jolt of understanding. Judging by Adam's expression, he felt it too. 'The list,' Jason whispered.

Adam pulled out his wallet and yanked a faded piece of paper from the billfold.

'I kept my copy in the same place,' Jason said. 'Right in my wallet – which was stolen by the crossbow killer. *He has this list!*'

'And Trinny's name is on it because we suspected she might be a vampire,' Adam went on. 'Since she's French, and she used to hang with Maggie sometimes.'

'So you were right about the killer being a vampire hunter. And we made his job a hell of a lot easier. We gave him a nice alphabetical list of vampires to kill!' Jason exclaimed in horror. 'Or at least a list of people you and I *thought* were vampires. Poor Trinny . . . It's our fault she's dead.'

'It's our fault they're *all* dead,' Adam replied.

'We've got to stop him before he kills again,' Jason said. He grabbed his tuxedo jacket off its hanger.

'If only we knew who his next victim was. He's probably stalking someone this very second,' Adam said, his fingers trembling as he tried to unfold the list.

'I already know the answer to that,' Jason said grimly, making for the door.

'How come?'

'The murderer is just going down the list,' Jason said. 'Killing vampires in alphabetical order. Think

179

about it . . .' He was running down the stairs now, with Adam racing after him.

'Dominic Ames, Scott Challon,' Adam murmured, still clutching the folded list. 'Trinny Dareau . . . Oh!'

Jason swung the front door open and as his eyes met Adam's he knew they were both thinking the same thing: Sienna Devereux was next.

FOURTEEN

'Let's go,' Jason said.

'Wait. Hold up!' Adam stepped into the doorway, blocking Jason's way. 'I know you're losing it at the moment, but you need to calm down. Maybe Sienna's not in any danger, at least not immediately.'

'She's next on the list. On *our* list—'

'I know,' Adam interrupted. 'But tonight is the full moon. The vampire-hunting season is over. The guy's already killed today. He's done. We have a few weeks before the next season begins, and we'll find a way to protect Sienna before then. We'll force Zach to believe us, and with him on our side . . .'

But Jason was already shaking his head. 'I don't buy it. This guy wants to kill vampires. He must have realized by now that Trinny *wasn't* a vampire. He made a mistake, and he'll want to fix it. He's only got tonight to do that.'

'You're jumping to conclusions,' Adam said.

'The last time he made a mistake was with me,' Jason pointed out. 'Then he murdered Dominic that very same day. He attacked a non-vampire, and when he realized his error, he killed an actual vampire only a few hours later.' Jason pictured Sienna, saw her with the crossbow bolt in her heart. 'He's going to do the same thing today.' He gently pushed Adam aside and headed for his car.

'Your mask!' Adam called, running after him with the hand-painted mask Dani had bought for Jason at the mall. 'They won't let you in without it.'

Jason skidded to a halt. 'And my ticket,' he muttered, patting his pockets. 'Where's the ticket? They really won't let me in without that.'

'Check your inside pocket,' Adam suggested.

Jason stuck his hand into the inner jacket pocket and felt the thin piece of parchment paper that the ticket was printed on. He was good to go.

'I can't go with you,' Adam panted as Jason slipped behind the wheel. 'I have to get dressed. They'll kick me out if I show up in jeans. The Sandhurst Castle doesn't allow jeans. Ever.'

Jason glanced at Adam's Vespa. 'I'll drop you home on my way to the castle,' he said. 'It will be faster.'

'It's true, the Vespa has never been the choice of an

action hero,' Adam said, climbing into the VW. 'And ever since you moved to town I seem to keep getting involved in crazy action-hero situations.'

Jason floored it, speeding toward Adam's house. As he drove, he fished his cell phone out of his pocket and dialed Sienna. 'Pick up, pick up, pick up,' he chanted as her cell rang. But instead of hearing her voice, he got the automated voicemail message. Jason hung up.

He screeched into Adam's driveway. 'Get there as soon as you can,' he said as his friend scrambled out of the car.

'I will. And, Jason, don't worry,' Adam said seriously. 'There are cops all over that place, whether you see them or not. Nobody's going to hurt Sienna.'

Jason nodded. But his fear only grew as he drove the rest of the way to the Sandhurst Castle. He had to force himself to stop at red lights and not to do 100 mph. Sienna was in danger and she didn't even know it.

When he reached the Sandhurst Castle, which was really just a big old mansion with a single turret, Jason slammed the car into park and leaped out with the engine still running. The valet had to jog after him to give him the ticket. Jason shoved it into his pocket and pushed through the heavy wooden doors of the building.

The place was filled with music. A string quartet dressed in black played at one end of the huge foyer. All four of the musicians wore white masks over their eyes. A swag of sheer golden fabric was draped from two columns on either side of the group, forming a canopy over their heads.

'Welcome and happy holidays,' said a woman in a deep burgundy evening gown. 'May I take your ticket, please?'

Jason stared at her, trying to figure out if he knew her or not. But the green feathered mask she wore covered almost her entire face. 'Um, sure.' He pulled the ticket out of his pocket and handed it to her as he scanned the hallway for Sienna.

'Not your valet ticket, your ticket to the ball,' the woman said, sounding vaguely annoyed, and suddenly Jason could place her. It was Sienna's mother. She always seemed a little annoyed by him.

'Mrs Devereux?' he asked. 'Where's Sienna?'

'I haven't seen her in a while,' Mrs Devereux replied. 'Your ticket?'

Jason dug out his ball ticket and handed it over. 'Have fun,' she called after him as he hurried up the marble steps and into the ballroom itself.

The place was huge, and every single inch of it was

beautifully decorated. Lush green pine trees lined the walls on either side, all decorated with golden bows and white lights. Some of the lights were large and some as tiny as little pieces of rice. The mixture of the two made the Christmas trees look magical, as if they were covered with a field of stars.

Burgundy velvet ribbons – the same shade as Mrs Devereux's dress – formed big bows on the back of each gold-upholstered chair. The tablecloths were the same burgundy color, with an overlay of the sheer golden fabric, and each table had a centerpiece of huge, fluffy ostrich feathers dyed to match the burgundy.

Feathers are ticklish, Jason thought, the memory of his IM conversation with Sienna popping into his head. His throat constricted and he felt a rush of fear. What if something happened to Sienna tonight, something bad? What if something had *already* happened?

Jason wove his way through the ballroom, searching for her. It wasn't very crowded yet, but everyone Jason passed was wearing a mask, making it impossible to see who they were. How was he supposed to find Sienna when the whole point of the evening was to hide your identity?

'Your mask doesn't work when it's in your hand,' a girl in a white dress with a deep V-neck called.

Jason stared at her, trying to place her voice. It wasn't Sienna's, but it was familiar. He looked at her eyes, hidden behind a smooth white mask that covered her whole face. The mask was a different kind of face, like a porcelain doll's, with one exquisite sapphire tear on its cheek.

The girl laughed, lifting the mask away from her face with the fancy carved stick that held it. It was Erin.

'You're supposed to wear it,' she said, taking Jason's mask from his hand. She slipped it into place over his eyes, and arranged the elastic band around the back of his head to hold it in place. 'Perfect,' she said, stepping back to admire him.

'Where's Sienna?' he asked, in no mood to make small talk.

'Wow. You really have it bad for her,' Erin laughed.

'I just need to find her. Now,' Jason said.

'She's off doing hostess stuff,' Erin told him with a shrug. 'Maybe she's talking to the chef or something.'

Jason moved on to the dance area, where multi-colored spotlights moved lazily across the wooden floor. There was more sheer drapery here, surrounding the whole dance floor so that it looked like a gypsy's tent. It was spectacular, but there was no sign of Sienna.

'Have you seen Sienna Devereux?' Jason asked

Dani's friend Billy, who was wearing a tuxedo and a mask shaped like a swan, its long, graceful neck curving over his head.

'Nope. Where's your sister?' Billy asked.

'I don't know,' Jason murmured and continued on through the stained-glass French doors to the balcony that ran along the outside of the building.

Alabaster lanterns glowed softly in the darkness. A dark figure stood in the shadows. As Jason stepped closer, the man turned, revealing a tuxedo beneath an old-fashioned cape and a white mask that covered only half his face like the Phantom of the Opera's.

The hair on Jason's arms stood up, and a feeling of unease unaccountably swept over him. Was this mysterious loner the killer?

'Can I help you?' the guy asked, and Jason recognized his voice instantly. It was Brad.

Jason didn't feel like getting into it with Brad right now, so he just shook his head and went back inside. The room was beginning to fill up now. People stood in little clusters of two and three, all of them exquisitely dressed with spectacular masks.

But Sienna was nowhere to be seen.

Jason pulled out his cell phone and dialed her number again. Her voicemail picked up immediately, and Jason cursed under his breath. She wasn't answering her phone and it seemed she wasn't at the ball. Had the hunter found her already?

FIFTEEN

Jason's cell phone rang, the shrill notes interrupting his search. He answered it immediately. 'Sienna?'

'Nope,' said Adam's voice. 'But that answers my question. You haven't found her yet?'

'No. Are you here?' Jason asked.

'I just walked in. I'm in the foyer,' Adam replied.

'I'll be right there.' Jason hung up and hurried back to the foyer. He figured maybe Adam could point out which of the masked partygoers were undercover cops. Jason could get some of them to help him search.

Except that Sienna was in the foyer already. The second Jason got there, he saw her. There was no mask in the world that could keep him from recognizing Sienna, and his heart flooded with relief at the sight of her. The crêpe fabric of Sienna's gold dress clung to her curves, then widened into a frothy, delicate skirt that was cut dramatically to skim the ground at the back, while rising to just below her knees at the front. She stood talking to Adam and another guy.

'Freeman!' Adam called and waved.

Sienna turned to face Jason as he walked over to them. The mask she held up to her face was a stunning combination of antique white lace and gold enamel, the textured fabric braided into the smooth, shiny gold. It covered half her face, from her forehead down to her nose, with a large ruby set in the forehead between her eyes.

'Jason,' she said, lifting the mask away from her face. He noticed that the stick it was attached to had a red silk thread twisted around it, with a long feather dangling from the end.

'Feathers,' he murmured, smiling at her.

She smiled back. 'They're sexy,' she replied, her voice husky.

'Well, hello, Captain America,' said the guy standing with Adam and Sienna. 'Love the red, white, and blue.'

Jason gazed at him in surprise. It was Detective Tamburo, all decked out in a tux with his longish hair pulled back into a neat ponytail. He even had a mask, although his was a plain black leather eye mask.

'Huh?' was all Jason could think to say.

'Your mask,' the detective replied.

Jason glanced down at the mask. A field of red stars on a blue background, and a white stick to hold it with. 'Oh. Yeah. I hadn't noticed,' Jason said.

But Tamburo had already forgotten about Jason. 'The sooner we go, the sooner you'll be back,' he said to Sienna. 'You don't want to miss the whole ball after you planned it all, do you?'

'Go?' Jason cut in. 'Go where?'

'Detective Tamburo wants me to go to the police station,' Sienna sighed. 'Right in the middle of everything.'

'This killer isn't going to wait for you to finish your little masquerade, princess,' Tamburo said. 'And think how happy you'll be if you're the one to help put him away.'

'Do you have a new lead?' Jason asked.

The cop nodded. 'We've got a witness who can put a friend of Dominic's near the scene of his murder. Since his girlfriend's out of town, I'm hoping the divine Ms D. here can ID the photo for me.'

'Why can't I do it in the morning?' Sienna protested. 'Jason, tell him I can't leave my own party.'

'Actually, I think it's a great idea,' Jason told her. *A great idea that will get you out of harm's way*, he added silently. Then he could concentrate on catching the

191

murderer. He'd check the list to see who was next after Sienna, then he and Adam could alert the cops and they'd all be ready to pounce the instant the killer made a move. If he didn't have to worry about Sienna's safety, Jason knew he'd be able to focus a lot better. He shot a look at Adam.

His friend took the hint.

'It's true, Sienna. If you can recognize the guy, maybe you'll get a killer off the street,' Adam put in. 'The party can wait.'

'I promise, it will be worth it,' Tamburo told her.

'If I ID this guy in a photo, how long will it take you to find him?' Sienna asked.

Tamburo shrugged. 'Hey, I'm good, but I can't see the future. You got a crystal ball, princess?' He glanced at Jason. 'Although I guess that's more your department, isn't it, Freeman?'

The sound of hundreds of tiny bells chiming at once filled the cavernous foyer.

'It's time for dinner to start. Everyone please find your tables!' Sienna's mother called. Jason spotted Dani and Kristy in the throng of people heading toward the ballroom.

'Let's go,' Detective Tamburo said, taking Sienna's arm. 'I'll have you back by dessert.'

They walked off toward the valet desk, and Jason turned to Adam. 'We need the list,' he said. 'If the killer can't get to Sienna tonight, he'll go for whoever is next.'

'How do you know? Have *you* got a crystal ball?' Adam joked, pulling the list out of his wallet. 'Didja pick one up at the psychic fair?' He began reading the names on the list aloud, but Jason wasn't listening.

'Wait a minute,' he interrupted Adam. 'Did you tell anyone about me going to the psychic fair?'

'What? No,' Adam said. 'Anyway, if not Sienna, then the next vampire—'

'Are you sure?' Jason interrupted again. 'You didn't tell your father? Or any of the cops?'

'That you're a new-age, crystal-toting weirdo?' Adam said. 'No. Who cares? We've got bigger things to worry about right now than your super-cool image, dude.'

'I'm not worried about my image!' Jason snapped. He took off after Tamburo and Sienna.

Adam hurried to catch up. 'Where are we going?'

Jason didn't answer. His eyes scanned the people drifting in from outside. Tamburo and Sienna were nowhere to be seen, but he had to find them. Jogging out onto the circular driveway, he finally spotted Tamburo – pulling away in his car, Sienna in the passenger seat.

'Damn,' Jason muttered. Just as Adam caught up to him, Jason turned and strode back inside. His pulse was hammering in his ears. Tamburo had teased him about having a crystal ball. About that being Jason's 'department'. But why would he say something like that . . . unless he happened to know that Jason had been to a psychic fair?

'Freeman, what's going on?' Adam cried, following him back inside.

Jason frantically searched the faces, looking for his sister. 'I can't recognize anyone with all these masks,' he complained. 'Where's Dani?'

'You have to look for the mask, not the person,' Adam said. 'Dani has that green mask with the cat ears . . . there!' He pointed out Danielle, stepping through the ballroom doors with Kristy and Billy.

Jason sprinted over to her, gently pushing masked party-goers out of the way in order to reach his sister.

'Dani,' he cried, grabbing her elbow. 'Wait. I need to know if you told anyone about the psychic fair.'

'Told anyone what?' she asked, looking over her shoulder as her friends disappeared inside the room.

'That I was there,' Jason explained impatiently.

'Oh. No. I wouldn't do that to you.' Dani took her arm away from him. 'Why are you being so weird?'

'Did Kristy tell anyone?' he asked. 'It's important, Danielle. Do you know if she told *anyone at all* that I was there?'

'No. Of course she didn't tell. I'm sure.' Dani pulled her mask away from her face and frowned at him. 'Seriously, what's up with you?'

'Nothing,' Jason told her. 'Don't worry about it.'

'Well, you're a jerk,' Dani said mildly. 'Now I have to find my table on my own. I've totally lost Kristy and Billy in the crowd.'

'I can help you find it,' said a tall guy with a mask that looked vaguely Egyptian. It covered his entire face. 'It would be my pleasure.'

Danielle gazed up at him for a moment. 'Do I know you?'

'Not yet,' the guy said. He offered her his arm, and Dani took it with a smile. They walked off together without a backward glance.

'OK, spill,' Adam said when she was gone. 'What's the deal with the psychic fair?'

'No one knows I was there but Dani, Kristy and you. But Tamburo's joke implied that he knew too,' Jason said.

'But if nobody told him, how can he know?' Adam asked.

'There's only one way,' Jason said grimly. 'He found the ticket stubs – which were in my wallet when the crossbow killer took it!'

'You mean . . .' Adam blanched.

'Tamburo is the crossbow killer,' Jason said. 'He's the vampire hunter. And he's going to kill Sienna.'

SIXTEEN

Jason practically flew out of the castle. 'Keys,' he snapped at the closest valet. He fumbled in his pocket, pulled out the ticket and thrust it at the guy in the white jacket. 'Just the keys. I see my car. I'll get it.' He shoved a twenty into the dude's hand to get him motivated, and the guy quickly turned toward a board full of keys and started looking for Jason's.

The valet threw him his keys just as a hand clapped down on Jason's shoulder. Instinctively, Jason wrenched himself away and spun around to see Brad, without the mask this time.

'Freeman,' he said. 'We need to talk. I—'

'Later,' Jason interrupted, running for his car. He leaped into the Bug, slammed the key into the ignition and powered out of the lot. At least there didn't seem to be much traffic on the roads.

Which way am I supposed to turn? Jason wondered when he reached the Pacific Coast Highway. *Where is*

Tamburo taking her? One thing he was sure of was that they definitely weren't heading for police headquarters. But that's where Sienna thought she was going, so Jason decided to head toward the station. He was betting that Tamburo would at least start out in that direction so that he wouldn't panic Sienna right off.

He floored the gas, taking a yellow light and the very beginning of a red to a chorus of honks. OK, OK, there it was: Tamburo's anti-subtle, Vegas-baby 1967 Eldorado. The tail-lights were still quite a way ahead of him, but they were pretty distinctive. He was sure it was the right car. Jason let up on the speed and let the Bug slide in behind an SUV. He didn't want Tamburo to spot him. He was going to need the element of surprise.

Tamburo turned inland at Las Flores Canyon Road. It wasn't exactly the way to get to the station – not the fastest way – but it wasn't exactly the wrong way either. Jason followed, losing his SUV cover. He slowed down a little more, letting a new-skool Bug in front of him.

Then Tamburo turned east, into the canyon.

Exactly the wrong way.

Jason could feel adrenalin rushing through his body as he followed Tamburo around the sneaky curves, climbing up the canyon. Where exactly was he taking

Sienna? How was she doing up there? She had to know something was very wrong by now. Jason sped up a little, hoping for just a glimpse of her.

As *he* put on a little speed, the Eldorado put on a *lot* of speed.

'Crap!' Jason muttered, realizing Tamburo had spotted him. There was only one thing to do. Jason pushed down on the gas as far as he dared with the tight turns taking them higher and higher. Just a little faster, he told himself. Just a little bit faster. The Bug was a good car for taking curves, but Tamburo's boat of a car had a more powerful engine. The hills didn't slow it down at all.

Jason stamped down on the gas, silently urging the VW on, but it was no match for Tamburo's car. On the uphill, Jason fell further and further behind. Luckily, they reached a crest a few seconds later.

Now I can catch up, Jason thought.

He sped downhill, getting right on Tamburo's tail. There was no point in hiding now – it was clear Tamburo was on to him.

Tamburo pulled into the left lane on the two-lane road, away from the edge of the cliff, and pushed the Eldorado even harder. Jason raced after him, determined not to lose the bigger car. Tamburo braked to take a curve and the Bug slid up alongside. Jason shot a quick glance over at Sienna. She was gripping the dashboard with both hands and she was shouting something at the killer, but she was OK .

A pair of headlights came around the corner, heading straight for Tamburo. It was an 18-wheeler and it was thundering right at him.

Perfect, Jason thought. *Tamburo will have to slow down now.* Jason dropped back, allowing room for the Eldorado to pull back into the right lane in front of him. But Tamburo was too slow.

The Eldorado's brakes squealed as Tamburo braked and swerved at the last minute.

The 18-wheeler's horn let out a long, panicked blast.

Then the Eldorado spun, slid, flipped – and disappeared over the edge of the canyon.

SEVENTEEN

The truck driver either didn't see or didn't care what had happened to the Eldorado, because he carried on along the road, barely even slowing down. But Jason's hands shook on the wheel as he pulled the Bug over to the side of the road and stopped. He didn't bother with the door. He vaulted out of the convertible, ignoring the pain in his chest, and dashed over to the edge of the cliff.

His eyes went immediately to the Eldorado. It lay halfway down the hillside like a dead thing. The top had buckled and smoke was snaking out from under the hood. Jason realized that he had to get Sienna out of there in case the whole thing blew.

She's going to be OK, Jason told himself as he half-slid, half-scrambled down the cliff. The hillside was covered in the scrubby little bushes that dotted all the cliffs around Malibu and sharp branches scratched at Jason's legs, but he didn't care. All he cared about was

Sienna. *She has to be OK. She can survive anything but a stake through the heart, right?* he reminded himself. *She's going to be fine.*

Jason skidded to a stop next to the Eldorado and crouched down to peer in through the passenger side window. Sienna hung suspended by her seatbelt, her long hair hiding her face. His gaze slid lower, and that's when he saw the blood – so much blood! He couldn't see where it was coming from, but the front of Sienna's gown was soaked a deep crimson.

He looked past her, trying to see Tamburo. Was he conscious? It was impossible to tell.

'Hang on, Sienna!' Jason shouted, pounding on the window. 'I'm getting you out of there.' He thought she might have moved a little at the sound of his voice, but he wasn't sure.

He grabbed the door handle and yanked, bolts of pain shooting out from his chest wound. Then he realized the door was locked. Of course it was locked. What was he thinking?

'Sienna!' he yelled. 'You've got to unlock the door!' Sienna didn't move. Jason scanned the ground and grabbed the biggest rock he could find. He slammed it against Sienna's window again and again and again.

The acrid smell of something synthetic burning

filled his nose and worked its way down to his lungs. He realized that he didn't have much time. The car could go up like a torch at any second. 'Sienna!' Jason yelled again. And, suddenly, Sienna turned her face toward him.

'Unlock the door. I have to get you out of there!' Jason shouted. Her hand reached in the wrong direction. Jason tapped the spot where the lock was. 'You're flipped. It's up here.'

A few seconds later, Sienna had the door unlocked. Jason grabbed the handle and pulled. The door opened about a foot, then snagged in the dirt. Jason braced his foot against the car and pulled again. He felt the stitches in his chest rip open as he jerked the door inch by inch through the earth.

Finally, he thought he'd pried the door open far enough. The fumes searing his lungs, Jason leaned into the car. 'I've got you,' he murmured as he carefully unbuckled Sienna's seatbelt. She slid into his arms, unconscious, and as carefully and as quickly as he could, Jason maneuvered her body out of the car.

Sienna's blood soaked into the front of his shirt as he carried her away from the smoldering wreck. When he was sure that she was a safe distance away, he gently put her down. He let himself look at her for a long moment, then he turned back to the car. Fingers of flame were reaching out from under the hood. If he wanted to get Tamburo out, Jason knew he didn't have much time.

He was moving toward the Eldorado before he'd consciously decided to save the man. Jason didn't even know if Tamburo was alive *to* save, but actually it didn't matter. He had to at least try. The thought of leaving anyone to be burned alive made his stomach heave. If Tamburo survived, Jason figured he'd let the cops deal with him.

Jason had to crawl into the car himself to release the detective from his seatbelt. The smoke was thick inside the car now. The fumes felt as if they had replaced every molecule of oxygen. Jason couldn't tell if Tamburo was unconscious or dead as he dragged the man out of the car and away from the wreckage, and he didn't stop to check. All he wanted was to get Tamburo clear and get himself back over to Sienna.

He'd just about decided he'd got Tamburo far enough away from the car to be safe, when there was a *whomp* and a blast of searing air knocked Jason over as the car exploded. 'You're on your own,' Jason muttered to Tamburo, leaving the cop lying on the hillside behind a large boulder as he ran back to Sienna.

'You're going to be OK now,' Jason said as he dropped to his knees beside her. 'I'm here.' He was worried by the sight of all the blood. It looked as though Sienna's body had lost more blood than it could possibly have held! His eyes darted over her, looking for the source. Then he spotted a ragged cut on the inside of her right elbow. It had caught an artery, and she was losing blood so quickly that even the ability to heal super-fast, which Jason knew all vampires had, couldn't save her. Sienna was bleeding out.

Jason jerked off his shirt and used his teeth to start some tears in the fabric. Then he ripped off a few strips of the cloth. He could feel some of his own blood trickling down his chest from his wound, but he ignored it. He rested Sienna's wrist against his shoulder to elevate her arm while he bandaged it.

The bandage went red with blood almost instantly. Jason wrapped another strip of cloth over the first one. Then, remembering the first aid his old swim coach had taught the team, he wrapped a third strip of cloth around Sienna's arm and pulled it tight, in an attempt to push the artery closed against the bone in her upper arm. He must have been at least partially successful, because the bleeding seemed to lessen considerably.

Sienna's eyelids fluttered and she gave a soft moan, but she didn't regain consciousness.

Jason could see that Sienna needed help. Her face was drained of color, even her lips. And the second bandage was already turning red. He pulled his cell out of his pocket: zero bars – no service. He slid Sienna's cell out of the tiny purse she wore over her shoulder: smashed.

Jason stared at the top of the cliff. He could climb back up there, try to flag down a car. Maybe the driver of the 18-wheeler had even called for help. But he didn't want to leave Sienna.

What am I supposed to do? What in hell am I supposed to do? Jason wondered desperately. His heartbeat pounded in his ears. And, suddenly, he realized that he had the answer: his heartbeat, his blood! Sienna needed blood, and she had a particularly effective way of getting it.

Immediately, Jason brought his wrist to Sienna's lips. She didn't react.

'Sienna, bite me. Drink my blood. I *want* you to drink it,' he pleaded. He nudged her lips with his wrist. Nothing. Was she too far gone? Was she going to die right there in front of him?

Jason wasn't about to let that happen. He pulled his

car keys out of his pocket and reached for the little Swiss Army knife key chain. He flipped open the blade and used it to nick his wrist. A few droplets of blood sprang to the surface.

Jason thrust his wrist in front of Sienna's mouth again. This time her lips twitched. Then she bit into him and began to feed, fast and hard, drawing the blood out of his veins.

It was nothing like the time Erin Henry had fed on him. Jason hadn't been aware of the blood leaving his body then. He'd just felt dizzy and drunk and ... ecstatically oblivious. This time he was aware of the small sharp pain of Sienna's teeth piercing his skin, of his blood racing through his veins at an accelerated speed. And it was slightly terrifying. *She needs this,* Jason reminded himself. *She has almost nothing left.*

Sienna's dark eyes snapped open. She stared up at Jason blankly, and he wasn't sure if she recognized him. Was it shock? Jason wondered whether, in her current condition, Sienna would be able to stop. Maybe she needed so much blood that she would have to keep drinking now. Would she be taken over by the blood-lust? Would she drain him completely?

He thought about pulling away, but he didn't know how to tell if she'd had enough. He had to trust her. *She will stop, won't she?* he thought, starting to feel slightly lightheaded himself.

Sienna's sharp teeth didn't release his wrist.

Jason tried to say her name, but a wave of dizziness spun him away. Blackness crept into the edges of his vision and he felt himself sliding into unconsciousness . . .

EIGHTEEN

Jason felt Sienna jerk her head away from his wrist. Slowly his vision cleared and he struggled back to consciousness. He looked anxiously down at Sienna and was relieved to see that pink had seeped back into her lips and cheeks. She brought her fingers to her mouth and held them up in front of her. They were stained with a few drops of his blood. 'What did I do?' she whispered, sounding horrified.

'What I wanted you to do,' he said quickly. 'What you needed to do. You and Tamburo were in a car crash. Do you remember? You'd lost a lot of blood.'

'But how much have I drunk?' Sienna asked. 'It must have been a lot.'

'I've still got plenty,' Jason told her. He thought it was true. His head felt like it was slowly bobbing up and down, but he was alive, and she was alive, and that was all that mattered.

He tossed her his shirt. 'You might need another

bandage on your arm. I need to go check whether Tamburo's still alive. Just rest, OK?'

Jason pushed himself to his feet and cautiously crossed the few feet to the killer. He'd seen a lot of horror movies and he half expected the man to suddenly leap to his feet and attack him. But Tamburo lay motionless.

'Hey!' Jason said, kneeling down and checking the side of Tamburo's neck for a pulse.

'Is he dead?' Sienna called. She was sitting up now, staring over at him, her face expressionless.

Jason kept his fingers pressed to the detective's neck for a few moments more, just to be sure. 'Yeah,' he answered at last. 'He's dead.'

Sienna let out a long, shuddering sigh as Jason walked back over to her. 'Adam was right about the crossbow killer being a vampire hunter,' she said. 'But even he didn't figure out that the killer was the detective who was supposedly *looking* for the killer.'

'How did you figure it out?' Jason asked.

'I didn't exactly have to,' Sienna admitted. 'It didn't take me long to realize we weren't going to the police station. When I asked Tamburo why, he just told me. He said I was going to make the perfect kill for the full moon. He wanted to come out here to do it right. I guess there's some kind of ritual or something. The guy was seriously whacked.'

'Tell me about it,' Jason said, glancing down at his chest wound. It had mostly stopped bleeding.

'What I don't understand is how he knew to come looking for vampires here,' Sienna said. 'I mean, we've been in Malibu for generations, and no one's come after us before. We didn't even know there *were* any hunters.'

'I have an idea about that,' Jason admitted. 'I think maybe Tamburo knew about the chalice. I mean, it's a pretty ancient artefact. Maybe hunters try and trace items like that, hoping they'll lead to vampires. He could have been the guy who bought it, and when the pawnbroker said someone wanted it back, he probably guessed that someone would be a vampire. I think he was watching me the day I went to get the chalice back from the pawnbroker. I had a feeling at the time that somebody was.'

'So that's why Tamburo went after you in the first place,' Sienna said. 'He thought you were one of us – because you bought the chalice.'

'I think so,' Jason agreed, suddenly realizing there was something he ought to do. Quickly, he went back over to Tamburo and searched through the detective's pockets for the wallet the killer had taken from him. He soon found it – along with something else . . .

'Tamburo's receipt for the chalice is right here,' Jason told Sienna. 'So he obviously *was* the guy who bought the chalice from the pawnbroker originally.' He crumpled up the receipt as he walked over to Sienna. 'And this is my wallet that Tamburo stole from me,' he went on. 'And in it is this.' He handed her a folded piece of paper. 'It's a list of possible vampires that Adam and I made when we first discovered that there were vampires living in DeVere Heights.' He ran his fingers through his hair. 'I'm sorry, Sienna. We practically handed him your names and addresses.'

'Have you forgotten that you got shot too?' she asked gently.

'That's true. I wonder why Tamburo never tried to take another shot at me,' Jason said.

Sienna smiled. 'The amount of time you've been taking to heal from one little, tiny crossbow wound would have told him not to bother,' Sienna answered. 'You clearly aren't a vampire.'

Jason nodded. 'Good point!' he said. 'Now, give me that list.'

'Why?'

'Just give it.'

Sienna handed it to him. Jason took it and the receipt for the chalice and walked as close to the burning car as he could. He stared into the blaze for a moment, then tossed the two pieces of paper in. They were devoured instantly.

He considered adding the ticket stubs from the psychic fair to the fire, but decided not to. If you thought about it a certain way, his going to the psychic fair had saved Sienna's life – not because of Madame Rosa and her 'varning' of 'great danger', but because if Jason hadn't had those ticket stubs from the fair in his wallet, Tamburo wouldn't have made that comment about a crystal ball and Jason wouldn't have realized that Tamburo was the killer in time to stop him killing again.

That was not something Jason even wanted to think about. Instead he decided to keep the stubs right where they were. He felt he could use a good-luck charm. He believed in those, sort of.

'You think you can walk?' he asked Sienna when he returned to her. 'Because I'm pretty sure I can't carry you back up to the road.'

Sienna nodded. 'Maybe I should carry *you*,' she said as Jason helped her to her feet. 'I definitely think I should drive home. You look a little shaky.'

'Me? *You* were unconscious about ten minutes ago,' Jason replied as they slowly started to climb. 'There's no way I'm letting you drive the Bug.'

'But you know I'm superhuman,' Sienna countered, with a grin. 'I'm mostly healed up already.'

'Yeah, but I'm a guy,' Jason argued. Unfortunately, at that moment he stumbled and had to grab on to Sienna's arm to keep from falling on his butt.

She laughed. 'Yeah, you're a guy – a life-saving hero, but also a normal guy – which is why I should drive,' she told him as they reached the road.

'How does that make any sense? I don't know what you keep doing to your Spider, but how many times has it broken down since I've—?'

Jason broke off abruptly, distracted by a car pulling over to the side of the road behind his VW. The headlights were bright and they were shining right in his eyes.

'You two need a ride?' a familiar voice asked, and Brad stepped into view. His eyes widened with shock when he saw Sienna. 'Is that blood? What happened? Are you all right?'

'I'm fine,' Sienna told him. 'Jason gave me a little . . . transfusion.'

'What happened?' Brad repeated.

'The crossbow killer is down there – dead,' Jason said. 'Sienna was going to be his next victim.'

Brad sank down on the hood of his car. They all stared at one another silently for a moment. 'Tell me,' Brad said simply.

Sienna and Jason sat down next to him and answered as many of his questions as they could.

Finally Jason asked a question of his own. 'What are you doing out here, anyway?'

Brad grinned. 'I had this speech to make to you. More like an apology, I guess. I tried to talk to you at the ball, but you blew me off, so I decided to follow you. I didn't think I'd be able to have a good time until I'd said what I had to say. I got lost a few times – you were kind of hard to keep track of – but here I am.' Brad looked from Jason to Sienna, and then down to the burning Eldorado. 'Now it seems like it's maybe not the time for that conversation.'

'You don't have anything to apologize to me for,' Jason told him. Well, he kind of did, but Jason was willing to let it slide. It wasn't like Brad had tried to kill him or anything.

'Yeah, I do,' Brad answered. 'Sienna broke up with me because, for a long time, we've been more friends than anything else. We weren't in love like we used to be.' He looked down at the ground for a moment, then over at Sienna. 'It was true, but I didn't want to hear it. I thought – and I thought everyone else would think – she was dumping me because she'd found somebody she liked better. Basically, you,' he told Jason.

'Brad, I really meant it when I said it was about us, about how things were with us,' Sienna said softly.

'I know, but it took a while for that to sink in,' Brad replied. 'And while it was sinking in, I was a jackass.' He stuck out his hand. 'I'm sorry, Freeman. You have to accept my apology or the whole swim team will be on my back. Curt's missing his girlfriend. I don't think I can keep him at DeVere the whole semester.'

Jason grinned and shook Brad's hand. 'Accepted. And thanks.'

Brad opened the back door. 'You two get in. I'll be chauffeur.'

Jason slid into the car. Sienna gave Brad a quick hug and then slid in beside Jason.

'So, Freeman,' Brad said cheerfully as he pulled out onto the road. 'You look like crap.'

Jason laughed, then groaned. Even laughing hurt. 'Yeah, well, you guys aren't the easiest people to hang out with,' he said. 'What with the extra strength and the high pain threshold and all.'

'And don't forget our extreme good looks,' Brad joked.

'Luckily for me, I'm naturally gifted in that department,' Jason retorted.

'Yeah, that bruised and battered look is really working for you,' Sienna teased.

She was right about the bruised and battered. Every muscle in Jason's body ached. He was going to have to get new stitches. And he'd probably need to take iron supplements or something for his blood loss. But Jason felt great. His friendship with Brad was back on track, he'd saved Sienna's life, and the crossbow killer could no longer hurt anyone. But what made Jason happiest of all right now, was the feel of Sienna sitting right beside him – and the promise of all the possibilities that lay between them . . .